THE CASE
OF THE
PHILOSOPHERS'
RING

THE CASE
OF THE
PHILOSOPHERS'
RING

by Dr. John H. Watson

UNEARTHED BY RANDALL COLLINS

Crown Publishers, Inc.   New York

For Judy
who knows all about detective stories

Passages from the following titles are used by permission from the publishers.

Humanities Press Inc., New Jersey for lines from TRACTATUS LOGICO-PHILOSOPHICUS by Ludwig Wittgenstein.

Cambridge University Press, New York, for lines from PRINCIPIA ETHICA by G.E. Moore, 1903, reprinted 1971.

BOOK DESIGN RHEA BRAUNSTEIN

Some of the materials related in this book are true. Some anachronisms, and outright falsehoods as well, have been introduced for the sake of the story.

Library of Congress Cataloging in Publication Data

Collins, Randall, 1941–
    The case of the philosophers' ring by Dr. John H. Watson.

    1.   Russell, Bertrand Russell, 3d Earl, 1872–1970—
Fiction.   I.   Title.
PZ4.C7128Cas   1978   [PS3553.O476]   813'.5'4   78–12689
ISBN 0-517-53530-0

Editor's Preface

It was once thought the Holmes canon was closed. But scholarship has shown that this is not so, and that diligent searching through archives of old papers will turn up more narratives of the great detective. However, one must know what one is searching for, and I will admit to having convinced myself this book existed long before going to look for it. It came about in the following way.

I was studying the origins of the great revolution in philosophy that began early in the twentieth century, and which is even now sweeping the other disciplines before it. This was my occupation by day; at night, I will confess, I turned for relief to the Edwardian underworld. In one half of my life, I pored over the logical arguments of Russell and Whitehead, Moore and Wittgenstein. In the other half I lounged through the schemes and exploits of the occultist Aleister Crowley, of William Butler Yeats and the Order of the Golden Dawn, of the Theosophical Society and the Society for Psychic Research.

Yet for all my care, the two realms would not stay apart. The names began to come off the printed page. And as they came to life, the worlds they inhabited flowed into one: they all lived in the same world, and a rather close-knit one at that. They did not refer to each other in their works, but they knew each other in their lives.

Russell, the philosopher and epitome of good; and Crowley, the evil master of the occult: what could they have in common? But they attended the same college—Trinity College, Cambridge—at the same time; the one involved in scandals, leaving without taking a degree, the other progressing from intellectual glory to glory—but finally expelled from his position as well.

John Maynard Keynes, next door at Cambridge, whom Russell did not quite approve of, yet respected and frequented all the same—he led another set of double (or quadruple) lives: economist and logician in one compartment, financial speculator in another, with yet other connections behind closed doors that Russell did not care to open, but which closed nevertheless behind such as Lytton Strachey and Virginia Woolf.

And then there was Ramanujan, the strange mathematical genius from the mysterious East, brought to Russell's own Trinity College by Russell's staunch supporter, Hardy, only to die at just the time Russell was expelled from his fellowship, and just the time of Crowley's nefarious underground activities in the World War.

The lives kept flowing together, and, more to tell, their lives were troubled, and troubled in ways that linked too closely to be sheer coincidence. I became troubled myself, in my quiet and scholarly way. Why did they not speak to their interconnections, since connections there certainly were? Was there something to hide? Or was it something more, something unutterable? The more I pondered the question, the more certain I became that there was a mystery here to be solved.

The clincher was Wittgenstein, the man whom many people consider the greatest philosopher of the twentieth century, a man so strange in real life that one wonders how he could ever appear in fiction. Alternately bold and furtive, Wittgenstein was a man with something to hide, if ever there was one. In his biography,* Wittgenstein is quoted as saying he much preferred stories about detectives over any other form of writing. He was obviously indebted to one, I thought.

The essential link came when I realized Wittgenstein was indeed involved with the occult underworld—he was a mystic. Russell, though, was not; what then was he doing so intimately connected with Wittgenstein? Then I realized that Russell *was* connected, but through another intermediary—Annie Besant, head of The Theosophical Society, Russell's co-worker in various political causes over the years. The Theosophical Society was the very organization that Crowley's first occult order, the Golden Dawn, had split from. Here then, more links, the heart of the mystery perhaps.

Finally it all came clear. I sat up in bed one night. I had the solution! Sir Arthur Conan Doyle was also a member. I knew what to look for now, and where to look. I shall not tell you exactly where I found the manuscript, but I can say that the old Theosophical headquarters on Avenue Road, London, was a beginning point, and eventually the manuscript was unearthed.

Is it truth? Is it fiction? Arthur Conan Doyle, the doctor with little practice and much time on his hands, alternating between psychical research and tales of a detective with a morphine needle; Russell, the fairy-tale lord of the mind and the soul, who believed in neither; Wittgenstein, the all-time archetype of the mad genius; Crowley, Holmes, Ramanujan, Keynes—all are equally improbable, all equally true to the deeper levels of life that show through only in the imagination. Of the whole array, there is only one person whose reality is solid, unimaginative, and incontestable. The one person with his feet on the ground, of course, is Dr. Watson. Without his testimony, I would not have believed this story. But with it, I can only say: God help us that such people should ever come to life again!

RANDALL COLLINS, Ph.D.

---

* Norman Malcolm, *Ludwig Wittgenstein: A Memoir* (Oxford University Press, 1958), pp. 35–36.

Contents

PART I. A SUNNY DAY

Chapter 1.   A Call to Cambridge   *2*
Chapter 2.   Pacifists and Fisticuffs   *6*
Chapter 3.   The Brains of Bertrand Russell   *11*
Chapter 4.   The Concerns of a Lady   *18*
Chapter 5.   Alice's Wonderland Garden   *23*
Chapter 6.   Ramanujan the Great   *33*
Chapter 7.   The Economics of John Maynard Keynes   *38*
Chapter 8.   An Unexpected Ally   *48*
Chapter 9.   The Missing Philosopher Returns   *54*
Chapter 10.   The Stroke of Death   *60*

PART II. IN DARKEST NIGHT

Chapter 11.   The Tale of the Cabbala   *72*
Chapter 12.   Crowley's Castle   *78*
Chapter 13.   The Wickedest Man in England   *82*
Chapter 14.   The Circle of the Damned   *95*
Chapter 15.   An Astral Spy   *103*
Chapter 16.   Clouds and Shadows   *112*
Chapter 17.   The Mark of the Beast   *123*
Chapter 18.   Russell in Jail   *132*
Chapter 19.   Confrontation of the Mages   *138*
Chapter 20.   The Lord of the Ring   *148*

Epilogue   *151*

PART ONE

A SUNNY DAY

CHAPTER 1

A Call to Cambridge

Sherlock Holmes's intellectual talents, although extraordinarily acute, were narrowly attuned to matters useful for the detection of crime. Yet I have had occasion to mention, time and again in these narratives, the predilections for pure scholarship that would seize him at odd times, when the criminal world offered nothing to absorb him. For his bent of mind, it seemed, the more obscure the topic the better, and he would appear as the most withdrawn antiquarian, absorbed in the details of deciphering medieval codicils or charting the sixteenth-century formalities of the motets of Lassus. His distance from the clamors and debates of the current intellectual scene was so immense that he might as well have been still absorbed in his old habit of injecting himself with morphine. All the more surprising, then, were these events that took place in the year just before the Great European War, in which Holmes not only appeared at the center of that intellectual world he abhorred, but even played a part in it that changed the intellectual history of the twentieth century.

These remarkable events began on a beautiful spring morning in May.

"Great Scott, Holmes!" I began, looking out the window of our Baker Street lodgings. "The sun is shining, the haze is dispelled. Such a day in London comes hardly once a year. Surely you could pull yourself away this morning for a stroll along the Serpentine?"

"The Serpentine," said Holmes dryly, "is but an idle meandering stream compared to the events that are afoot. Read this, Watson."

And he tossed a telegram across the breakfast table.

A GREAT MIND IS BEING STOLEN. PLEASE COME AT ONCE. RUSSELL, TRINITY COLLEGE, CAMBRIDGE

"What can this possibly mean?" I exclaimed. "A brain preserved in formaldehyde at the university laboratory is being stolen? What conceivable use could anyone have for such a thing, once its vital spirits are gone? And if it is only now being stolen, rather than already gone, this man Russell has only to put out his hand to arrest the blackguard before he carries off his precious jar. No, no, Holmes, for once you are being trifled with. This is a springtime undergraduate prank. Let it not deter us from our walk—if not at the Serpentine, at least, I beg you, in Green Park."

"There I have you, Watson," Holmes returned. "Unless I am very much mistaken, Russell is no undergraduate, but Bertrand Russell, the younger brother of an Earl, grandson of the late Prime Minister Lord John Russell, Fellow of the Royal Society and of Trinity College, Cambridge, and the most eminent mathematical philosopher of our day."

"You amaze me, Holmes," I cried, edging despairingly from the sunny window. "A mathematical philosopher, indeed! I had no idea your interests extended to this kind of thing. I myself have heard you many times refer to it as useless rubbish."

"The twentieth century is a new era," said Holmes. "There are new currents flowing in the best minds these days, and our scientists and philosophers of Cambridge are in the thick of it. Have you not heard of the splitting of the atom by that chap Rutherford? And Russell, with his friend Whitehead, has recently published a work in which they have, so to speak, split something far more difficult: they have split our system of numbers into the fine particles of pure logic. They have spent two hundred pages alone before getting to the number one."

"And split brains as well, Holmes? Have we now developed a method to chip off a little from a man's brain, bit by bit, like a Stilton cheese? The whole business speaks of nothing but the deterioration of our faculties. Split atoms, split logic, indeed!"

But Holmes was on his feet, adjusting his familiar deerstalker cap, and I found myself involuntarily following him to the door.

"Come, come," said Holmes. "You shall have your day in the sunshine, Watson, but you shall have it in the green gardens of the cloistered Fellows of Cambridge University, and not with the pompous idlers of Green Park. We have just time to catch the 8:47 from King's Cross Station."

Holmes was in a bright mood as we rode rapidly in a cab through the London streets, and he went on with unusual good humor.

"So you doubt that a mind can be stolen, my dear fellow. Have you not heard of the new psychic sciences, whereby a mind can be sucked out of a body like egg whites from an eggshell? Why, a psychic operative might have yours or mine at any time, if he saw any value in taking it."

"My skull is not an eggshell, I assure you," I replied, "and I should hope yours is not. I am sure I cannot say about Mr. Bertrand Russell's."

"Russell's brains are of as fine a stock as one might find in all of England," returned Holmes. "We live in a nation of some forty millions, but in matters of importance we need concern ourselves with only a few. And if such brains are in danger, or those related to them by blood or personal connection, then it is our duty as Englishmen to help."

"Do our duty we shall," I declared. "If your psychic sciences and your split logics leave anything for us to investigate. Not to mention this scientific craving to select the elite of the nation by genetics, while all the rest of us go hang. Your new sciences will end by breeding us like animals, selecting out the pure blood and eliminating the impure, as advocated by that man Galton."

"Precisely so," said Holmes coolly. "Sir Francis Galton has proven quite statistically that genius is hereditary, and he himself clearly illustrates his own principles. His own genius is indisputable; he has founded half a dozen sciences, including eugenics and psychometrics, as well as fingerprinting for the detection of crime, and the study of the cranial sizes of the lower social orders. And he himself is of impeccable heredity. His cousin was Charles Darwin—another old Cambridge man, by the way—and he shares with him as grandfathers the great botanist Erasmus Darwin and the artist Josiah Wedgwood."

"Sir Francis Galton shares at least two features with you, Holmes," I replied, "his intelligence, and his contempt for the common opinions of mankind. I've heard of the row he made when he went about the streets with a watch and cane, poking people in order to measure their reaction times."

"And there's a third point in common," said Holmes, sitting back with his pipe.

"A third point?" said I. "What is that?"

"Common blood," said Holmes. "Francis Galton is my uncle."

And with that, he said not another word until we reached Cambridge.

CHAPTER 2

Pacifists and Fisticuffs

We did not find quite the peaceful college-town atmosphere at Cambridge we had expected. Along the street from the station the shops were closed and shuttered, although here and there someone peeked furtively from behind a curtain. The streets themselves were deserted, and pieces of litter were strewn everywhere. There were shouts and trampling noises in the distance, in the direction of the colleges.

"What can it mean, Holmes?" I exclaimed. "Has the town been invaded by some wild beast?"

Holmes, like a bloodhound, was rapidly poking through the trail of debris. "That wildest of beasts, the human mob, Watson. Look here!" He indicated in the trash with his stick a broken piece of placard with the word PEACE, and another that read WAR IS NOT THE ANSW, while a third said BOSCH-LOVERS DIE! All around were rocks and broken glass, pieces of torn clothing, and a large wooden club with an ugly protruding nail.

"I should say there has been some kind of political rally, and perhaps a march, which has been attacked by its opponents and turned into a rout," Holmes continued, striding briskly toward the corner. "The line of retreat follows this lane, and ends, unless I am greatly mistaken, just here."

We came out suddenly into the road before the walls of Trinity College. There at the great medieval gate was a crowd, packed too close for the flinging of rocks, but pushing and scrambling in considerable agitation. A small group of gentlemen and women, their clothes rather in disarray, were pressed against the wall by a larger mob in the plainer garb of the local populace. The pacifist demonstrators, for such I took them to be, were not defending themselves, but endeavored to slip through the little postern gate on the side and through the corridor to the courtyard beyond. Their main defense was a line of women, who interposed themselves and their umbrellas between the gentlemen and the mob, which seemed torn between the desire to attack right through these bluestockings and a hesitation about striking women. A small group of policemen stood by watching the struggle. They made no effort to intervene, but seemed uneasy about the role of the women, and occasionally a bobby would shout some discouragement when unnecessarily violent hands were laid upon one of these ladies.

The policemen's worries were deepened by a fat man with a ruddy face, dressed formidably in top hat and frock coat, who stood just inside the gate and shouted a continuous string of orders. He seemed particularly concerned that none of the women should slip into the college, for as he repeatedly declared, "Public visiting hours must be observed! Ladies are forbidden in college before the hour of two o'clock in the afternoon, and after the hour of five. Policemen, do your duty! The law must be observed. Visiting hours are from two to five o'clock only in the afternoons, High Church holidays only excepted."

Despite the confusion of the scene, Holmes calmly lighted his pipe and approached the nearest of the officers.

"Good morning," said Holmes. "We are expected by Mr. Bertrand Russell, a Fellow of this college. Will you kindly see us through?"

The bobby tipped his cap to Holmes's commanding presence, but then a scowl crossed his face. "I beg your pardon, sir, but you may find Mr. Russell occupied at the moment. That's him, there, in the midst of this pack of agitators." He gestured toward a small, slender man in the melee. With a look of impeccable dignity, and despite a torn collar and missing hat, Russell was struggling for the gate while a couple of young farmers tore at his coat and a husky squire swung a riding crop at his head.

"Indeed," said Holmes coolly. "Perhaps with your assistance both Mr. Russell and ourselves might pass through this congestion into the quiet of his rooms."

The police sergeant, who seemed to put all his energies into maintaining a posture of stout immobility, looked over at us suspiciously. "Just a minute. What's the nature of your business with Mr. Russell? You might be another peace agitator, for all I know."

"I assure you," said Holmes, "that neither war nor peace holds the slightest interest for me. I am Sherlock Holmes, the consulting detective, and my business, like yours, is purely professional. You may consult Inspector Lestrade, of Scotland Yard, should you have any doubt."

"Very good, sir," said the sergeant. "I confess I am relieved to hear it. But you must ask the vice-master for leave to enter under these circumstances. My authority ends here at the gate." And he indicated the fat man in the top hat behind the gate.

Just then a very pretty lady with curly red hair rushed from the crowd and seized the sergeant by the arm.

"You must help that man!" she declared. "They are going to kill him!" She pointed in the direction of Russell. His assailants had tripped him and were kicking him vehemently with their boots.

The cluster of policemen straightened up like a row of toy soldiers and stared over her head.

"But he is an eminent scientist!" she said.

Not a move.

"He is known all over the world!"

No answer.

"But," she cried, "he is the brother of an earl!"

At this, the bobbies wavered and looked doubtfully at their sergeant. He frowned deeply, and then strode forward with a deep pull on his whistle.

"All right, no loitering here! The fun is up, move on, now!"

And the line of bobbies pressed forward with their billy clubs, poking and pushing at the crowd, which slowly began to fade away. The pacifists hurried to safety. Russell regained his feet, and, seemingly little the worse for wear, slipped inside the gate. Some of the mob, resentful of this unexpected turn of events, pushed back against the police line, and soon the billies were swinging more vigorously and a few of the former attackers were now themselves bloodied.

The husky squire who had whipped Russell found himself up against the police sergeant, and he protested bitterly. "Wait now, peeler, you've got the wrong game! I'm no Bosch-loving Communist agitator. I'm an anti-Communist!"

"I don't care what kind of Communist you are," said the sergeant, and hit him again with his club.

The fight was on now in earnest, with blows given and taken on both sides. The pacifists no longer obscured the scene with their passivity—at least the men were gone, though a few of the ladies remained, and these no longer received any restraining protection from the police, who themselves had lost most of their restraint. Only the vice-master stood fast at the gate, crying over and over again:

"No lady visitors allowed until two o'clock. The morals of college shall not be violated! Two o'clock until five o'clock only."

The pretty red-haired lady was still in the midst of the fight, shepherding out the last stragglers of her side. Her umbrella flashed amid the swinging clubs of the police, and soon the battle seemed to swirl mainly around her. Her energies seemed to grow more fiery as the struggle closed in. At length, two policemen caught her by the arms, and a third wrenched the umbrella away. She hung limply while a fourth prepared a pair of manacles.

"I say, Holmes," I declared, "had we not better intervene? This is a most gallant lady, and she seems about to suffer a great injustice."

"One moment, Watson," said Holmes, his hand on his pipe. "I believe the lady has not yet exhausted her resources."

Holmes was right. The red-haired lady's limpness was temporary only. The policemen relaxed their grips. Suddenly she twisted her arms free, struck one bobby a piercing blow with the heel of her hand, sent another flying with an extraordinary kick, and dashed for Trinity Gate. Only the vice-master barred her way.

"No admittance, madame. Visiting hours..."

He was interrupted by a formidable little fist in the midst of his ponderous stomach. He staggered back, and she dashed inside.

The vice-master lumbered after her, but he was no match for her speed. In a moment both of them were lost down the passageway.

"I say, Watson," declared Holmes with a faint smile. "The entry is uncontested. Perhaps we now can keep our appointment with the eminent Mr. Russell?"

CHAPTER 3

The Brains of Bertrand Russell

Bertrand Russell was a man of forty, spare, willowy, with slicked-down graying hair and a dignified expression above his long neck that gave him the look of an intelligent crane. He welcomed us into his rooms overlooking a Trinity College courtyard and bade us sit down. He had changed into a new black frock coat and another long white collar, and the scuffle outside seemed a subject farthest from his mind.

We sat on a sofa flanked by two stately wing chairs; Russell stood before us by the mantelpiece. Across the room was a writing table with a surface of fine red leather. A stack of papers was piled neatly at one edge, a pen and inkstand stood at the other, while a single sheet of paper with a few lines written upon it cut a precise diagonal across the middle. Behind the table were a pair of tall lead-latticed windows, pushed open on their hinges to admit the fresh morning air, and deep blue curtains hung in measured folds on either side. A fine wood cabinet with glass doors contained a moderate-sized collection of books—mostly great tomes carrying the gold-embossed crest of the university press or the heavy leather bindings and Gothic lettering of the German publishers. The walls of the room were austere white and carried no paintings, just a trio of engravings from Piranesi's labyrinths.

"I am very glad you have come, Mr. Holmes," said Russell. "I have admired your detective work for your efforts to be precise, observant, and clear thinking. These qualities are very dear to me. I have devoted my life to their advancement, and I fear that they are now in considerable danger."

"What precisely is the nature of this danger?" said Holmes.

"It concerns especially a young philosopher, Ludwig Wittgenstein, newly arrived here from Vienna. He is a most remarkable man, and his ideas are of the greatest importance. I think it is no exaggeration to say that the future of philosophy is in his hands. And now he is subject to an insidious menace from an unknown source."

"Has Wittgenstein been threatened physically?"

"I am not sure. He is very suspicious, and he seems to be on guard against something. But I think that the threat is rather more intimate, and that it operates mainly by preying upon his mind. He usually comes to my rooms at midnight and paces furiously back and forth without saying a word. Sometimes he will go on like this for hours. I have had to stand there with him, for it seemed very probable to both of us that if I sent him home he would commit suicide."

"Is that principally what worries you?"

"Only partly. There are a number of small signs that lead me to believe that Wittgenstein is coming gradually under some indefinable but evil influence. He is growing increasingly preoccupied, increasingly irritable. He is suspicious of almost everyone, but for what cause, I cannot say. If it were one particular problem, this matter would not be so troublesome, but it is more nebulous and more sinister. That weighs rather heavily on me, a lover of clarity. I should prefer to see the world in the light of a fine day at noon, and this is rather more like early morning when one is not quite awake. I am sure something is wrong. I can read the signs here, as plainly as I can see that all of Europe is preparing for a great war, and that in preparing for it we shall make things so that only a spark is needed to set it off."

"What can you tell me of Wittgenstein's background?"

"Very little, I fear. I mentioned he is from Vienna. His father is, I believe, an engineering manufacturer, and he himself studied in the engineering faculties at Berlin and Manchester before coming to Cambridge. I believe he came because he heard I could answer some of his questions regarding mathematics."

"And so he is a recent convert to philosophy."

"Yes."

"And as to the nature of his work, doubtless he has taken up the propositional logic you have introduced in your *Principia Mathe-matica*, and has made some valuable extension of it."

"That is correct," said Russell. "Let me explain the importance of what he has done. The purpose of philosophy is to arrive at absolute certainty, and I have always looked up to mathematics as the most certain principle in our world. Hence I was much disturbed, some years ago, to discover that there are many things in mathematics that are not proven at all, but must be taken on faith. I and my friend Whitehead set out to remedy this situation, and after many years of hard work we succeeded in part. We have carefully deduced a great deal of mathematics from a clear logical foundation. The work has encountered certain obstacles, I admit, and Whitehead has recently deserted the cause. And I do not feel myself fully capable of carrying on."

Here Russell bent forward slightly, as if under the burden of a great weight. Then he threw back his shoulders and continued. "It is exceedingly fortunate that Wittgenstein arrived at just this time, and that he has taken up the task, and in a new and very important direction. He proposes to apply the logical method not only to mathematics but to ordinary language itself, and to derive all possible verbal expressions from certain irreducible atomic facts. If he succeeds, it will be an enormous step forward in the discovery of absolute truth. For if mathematics is the language of science, ordinary words are the language of everything else. What Wittgenstein is doing will make a philosophic revolution of his-toric proportions. It will outdate the work of many centuries."

"And you think that someone might wish to prevent this from happening?"

"I am not yet persuaded by any one interpretation. If philosophy can have revolutions, it can have Establishments, too, and it is quite within the realm of political precedent, at least, for a crumbling regime to stick at nothing to preserve itself before the inevitable. Yet we carry on our intellectual battles with rather more ethereal weapons—at least I should hope we do."

"Has Wittgenstein any enemies?"

"Enemies?" said Russell. "He is rather an abrasive personality, but you may find that Cambridge is tolerant of a great deal of personal peculiarity. One may live here in the Middle Ages, if one likes, or in the world of Utopian schemes, and no one will mind very much. Though Wittgenstein is, I think, looked on with disfavor by some of the older dons."

"Because of his ideas?"

"No, because he refuses to wear a necktie at High Table. He was once reprimanded by the vice-master, and he has since refused to eat at Hall, and takes all his meals in his rooms. But these enemies, if such you call them, are figures of fun only. The same vice-master is a fanatic for dress. He once answered a fire alarm in college in the middle of the night, wearing a top hat and swallow-tailed coat."

"Yet there may be more serious antagonists." Holmes stepped to the mantel and drew his curved briarwood pipe from his pocket. "I have heard that there are sometimes quite cutthroat competitions in academic life concerning questions of intellectual priority."

"It is true," Russell frowned. "Newton and Leibniz, and their partisans, carried on a battle over their respective priorities in inventing the calculus that went on for a century. Yet Wittgenstein himself seems unconcerned with danger from that source. I have heard him declare that it is unlikely that anyone should think of something in his subject of which he had not thought already."

"I see," said Holmes, looking carefully at the bowl of his pipe as he stuffed it with tobacco. "We seem to be arriving principally at negative conclusions. Yet you are convinced there is a danger to philosophy, and to Wittgenstein in particular. You intuit, from various signs, that Wittgenstein is in danger of losing his mind, and that this is happening from some external influence. Can you give me any further grounds for your suspicions?"

"To put it strictly, I cannot. Yet my sense of this influence is so strong as to make a palpable impression on me. I hope, Mr. Holmes, that you do not doubt me when I say that I consider this a matter of the utmost seriousness."

"I do not doubt your sincerity," said Holmes. He lit his pipe and carelessly tossed the match into the fireplace. "But let me expose the matter in a different light. You feel strong influences at work. Is it so certain that they are aimed at Wittgenstein, or solely at him?" He looked up quickly at Russell. "Is it not possible that you yourself are the target?"

Russell looked surprised for the first time in the interview. He craned his ostrich neck still higher, and looked down at us from a bemused distance.

"A remarkable idea, Mr. Holmes."

"Have you no enemies yourself?"

"I hope not. Although on further consideration, perhaps I should hope so. It is a wicked thought, no doubt, but the world seems to be growing rather more wicked than once I supposed. My political activities on behalf of world peace, I fear, are not exceedingly popular in some quarters."

"We have seen it for ourselves," said Holmes. "But is it not true, you are devoted to politics quite as much as to philosophy?"

"Politics?" said Russell. He waved his hand deprecatingly. "It is, I fear, a deeply inbred reflex. It is a family tradition, as philosophy is not. My grandmother has greeted me with the words: 'Why Bertie, I hear you have published *another* book!' with a tone as if to say she heard I had just been convicted for sodomy. But no, I cannot see that it has any bearing upon the intellectual matters that I called you about."

"Do you have no intellectual antagonists?"

"I have convinced rather few persons of my opinions, although I am satisfied myself that in some matters I have arrived at ultimate truth. But no, Mr. Holmes, it is hard to see a personal danger from such sources. You must understand that I am not much given to pure intellectual pursuits these days."

"You are devoting yourself largely to politics?"

"I hope I can do some good in that arena. When I was very young and intelligent, I worked exclusively at mathematics. After I grew too old for the mental effort, I turned to philosophy. And now, having exhausted my brains almost entirely, I have turned to politics."

"I perceive that you jest, Mr. Russell."

"Not entirely. In all seriousness, I discovered a contradiction* at the very beginning of my work on the foundations of mathematics that threatened the whole system, and that taxed my brain

---

* This is the famous "Russell's paradox": Is the class of all classes which are not members of themselves a member of itself? If yes, no; if no, yes. —Ed.

continuously for four years. It was exceedingly disagreeable. I
eventually discovered what appeared to be the basis of a solution.
In all, I spent ten years working out the bones of the system, and
when it was done I felt I would never be capable of such intense
concentration again. My brain feels burnt out, Mr. Holmes. Only
the four walls are left standing, and some charred remains."

"You say your collaborator Whitehead has abandoned the
enterprise. Was there a strain in your relationship?"

"Not in any personal sense. Whitehead is an entirely unworldly
man. He is the son of a country parson, and he still uses that
ecclesiastical tome, *History of the Council of Trent*, as his bedside
book."

"Is there no jealousy between you?"

The ostrich neck jerked up again. "I think not. Are there
grounds for inferring such a thing, Mr. Holmes?"

Holmes waved his pipe abstractedly at the ceiling. "It is customary, Mr. Russell, for joint authors of a book to list their names
in alphabetical order, unless one author is plainly the major influence. And yet, in your *Principia Mathematica*, you list the authors
as Whitehead and Russell, although one hears the doctrine it
contains referred to generally as Russell's. From this I infer that
there is some personal delicateness between you, and that you are
at pains to mollify him."

The ostrich neck arched still more tautly, and then, reaching
some inner peak, returned to normal. "You are very acute, Mr.
Holmes. Yet I would wish to say no more of this matter, save that
Whitehead was my senior here at Cambridge, and that he proposed me for election into the Apostles."

"The Apostles?"

"It is a society that meets on Saturday evenings for free-ranging
discussions of any and all subjects. It dates back to the time of
Hallam and Tennyson. When first I joined as an undergraduate
some twenty years ago, it served as a place for free discussion of
religion, at a time when the college required profession of faith in
the Church of England, and we were feeling our way toward
atheism. Since then it has undergone a shift toward the breaking
of some rather different taboos, under the not entirely wholesome
influence of Keynes and Strachey."

"I take it that membership is not generally open to all?"

"On the contrary, it is very select. There was a year, somewhat before my time, when it had but one member. He held the weekly meetings, read the ritual and made the toasts by himself, even nominating new members and blackballing them as unsuitable. Eventually, as you can infer, he found some nominees who passed muster, and the society has survived and prospered."

"Is Wittgenstein a member?"

"He was invited, but refused to come. For this, I am afraid, he is cursed every meeting at the reading of the roll."

"And does he hold this curse against you?" said Holmes.

"He does not know of it. It is a game of ritual and secrecy. The very existence of the society is not supposed to be known to outsiders. I fear we are only large-brained children, but it is a wholesome pleasure. Wittgenstein does not believe in either pretence or pleasure."

At this, Holmes knocked the ashes from his pipe and made as if to leave.

"Will you take the case?" said Russell. "Philosophy is like swimming, you see. There is a natural tendency to float to the surface, and it takes great efforts to stay in the depths. I fear there are no others who can do it, if the best hopes of Cambridge are destroyed."

"The case does present one or two points of interest," said Holmes. "And I would not like to disappoint a personage of your distinction. Tell me, where is Wittgenstein now?"

"He lives in Nevile's Court. I would show you there, but I have set myself an inalterable minimum of writing ten pages each day, and I have yet to finish. Also, the visit would not prove entirely satisfactory."

"Why not?" said Holmes.

"Wittgenstein has disappeared. He has not been seen these past five days."

CHAPTER 4

The Concerns of a Lady

We descended the stairs and crossed the secluded inner courtyard. At the passageway that led to another wing of the college labyrinth, Holmes put a restraining hand upon my arm.

"Wait, Watson. There is more here than meets the eye."

He gestured back across the court. We could plainly see Russell's windows on the third floor, and those of the neighboring rooms to the left, as well as those on each landing of the stairwell between them. We ourselves could not be seen in the shadows of the passageway.

Russell sat at his desk, a look of deep abstraction upon his face. Then he abruptly rose, paced to the door, and sat down again.

"Nothing so strange about that, Holmes," I remarked. "The man has just had a harrowing experience, for all his aplomb. He might well be more agitated than this."

"Perhaps so," said Holmes. "But kindly observe the second floor window to the left of the stairs."

It seemed to be the room of some undergraduate, at the moment empty as its inhabitant attended a lecture or some other college function. Then someone moved inside, and I caught a flash of red hair.

"By Jove, Holmes, you are right. It is she, the lady pacifist."

18

"Not so pacifist at that, if you will remember precisely," said Holmes. He smiled and pointed again.

The red hair was gone now from the left second-floor window. Then it flashed brightly past the stair landing between the second and third floors. She was evidently heading for Russell's rooms. And he seemed to be expecting her, for he had left his desk and paced again to the door.

Yet minutes passed, and nothing happened. The door did not open; Russell did not move. At length he left the door and crossed the room. He disappeared from sight, then reappeared at the other window, in the bedroom to the far right.

The red-haired lady was nowhere to be seen. Then I saw some movement in the landings above. An undergraduate had left his rooms on the fourth floor and was passing down the stairs. I watched him successively at each landing, and then he passed out the door and across to the far end of the courtyard, where there was a passageway opposite the one in which we stood.

"Now where has she gone?" I muttered.

"Third-floor window to the left," said Holmes. Sure enough, there was the flash of red hair, but at the door. She was just leaving. But she did not appear in Russell's sitting room, and Russell himself remained visible alone at his bedroom window.

The red hair now passed the landing to the flourth floor, and in a minute I saw her go by the sitting room and bedroom windows just above Russell's. Then she disappeared again and, a few minutes later, reappeared in Russell's bedroom.

"Incredible!" I declared. "She must know a hidden passage."

"Or else she can walk through walls," said Holmes, puffing his pipe contentedly. "Observe, Watson."

Russell sprang to his feet. The red-haired woman seemed to remonstrate with him, and once or twice reached out her arms for him. Each time Russell backed away, and edged continuously toward the sitting-room door.

Holmes chuckled. "It is less important than I thought, Watson—merely a variant on an eternal human comedy. I have heard that Russell was rather a freethinker in matters of the relations between the sexes, though it appears here that his pupil is more apt to follow his own theories than he is himself."

Holmes turned to go, when a movement at the far end of the

courtyard caught his eye. A corpulent figure in a top hat was emerging from the opposite archway. It was the vice-master, and he too seemed to see the figures in Russell's bedroom window. For he strode grimly across to the stairs, and we caught glimpses of the top hat moving ponderously, though ever more slowly, up the landings.

But now Russell was at his desk in the sitting room again, and the red-haired lady was nowhere to be seen. The vice-master must have knocked at the door, for Russell rose to let him in. The top hat blustered angrily in the sitting room, then strode through the bedroom as Russell stood coolly by. The lady seemed to be gone.

"But where..." I began, but Holmes cut me off.

"Wait, Watson. Come this way." And he dashed down the corridor, through a little maze of courts and passages and out again into the open air where a narrow set of casement windows rose from the ground to the fourth story of a vine-covered wall. Sure enough, there was the red-haired lady, just about to leap from a ledge a few feet above the ground. She looked at Holmes and myself with a confident smile, and landed neatly just before us.

"Remarkable agility, madame," said Holmes. "May I ask whom I have the honor of addressing?"

"Not so very remarkable," she replied. "Any woman could do it... indeed, any man could, if only they developed their innate abilities. As to your question, I am Annie Besant."

"Indeed," said Holmes. "You are Mrs. Besant, once so famous for your labor agitation, and now the head of the Theosophical Society, as successor to the remarkable Madame Blavatsky?"

"I am," said Annie Besant. "And I should ask the same of you, though my intuitions tell me that you are not a college don, and that you are a good man, for you are attached by rays of positivity to my friend Bertrand Russell."

"I am Sherlock Holmes, and this is my friend Dr. Watson. And you are right that we are friends of Russell. But what brings you into connection with him? It is a long way from occult philosophy to Russell's mathematical logic, or even to his political concerns with war and peace."

"The realm of light is at one against the forces of darkness, Mr. Holmes," she said melodiously. "Bertie is as yet very rational, and does not understand his powers of intuition, although he has a full complement of them. Hence he has special need at this time of a psychic guardian, when he takes so much upon himself, and exposes himself to so much negativity."

"What is this negativity that you sense?"

"Bertie and I have marched together on many a cause," said Annie Besant. "We have fought for the rights of the laboring poor, and for the rights of atheists and non-conformists to publish their opinions. We went through an election campaign when Bertie received as much abuse for advocating votes for women as he did today for advocating peace. So when I heard he would speak this morning to a public meeting, I felt he would need my presence. No, more than felt it—I *knew* it. And so I came."

"Most remarkable," said Holmes. "Can you describe more precisely the nature of this feeling?"

"It is a force much greater than ourselves, Mr. Holmes. Have you not felt it on occasion yourself?"

"I observe and think," said Holmes. "Feelings are superfluous to those tasks."

"Oh, but I know you will change soon," she said forcefully. "I have a feeling that you will experience this feeling before so very long."

"I shall await the experiment," said Holmes. "But tell me, was it this same feeling that prompted you to clamber down the vines from the fourth floor into the back window of Russell's private rooms?"

"You do not entirely approve, Mr. Holmes. Tell me, is it the vines for which you are so concerned, or that it should be a woman who climbs in to visit the man, instead of the old tradition that decrees it must only be the other way around?"

How Holmes would have answered this feminine onslaught I do not know. For just at that moment, a top-hatted figure appeared in the alley behind us.

"Stop, now! There, I have you at last. Are you unaware of the rules against female visitors? Two o'clock to five o'clock only, and most strictly, not in any college rooms, not to mention the rule prohibiting insults to the person of an official of college. I shall have you sent down! Were you a member of the college, but since you are not..."

The vice-master stopped, out of breath at the enormity of the outrages to his rules and his logic. Holmes and me he seemed scarcely to notice.

Annie Besant merely looked at him coolly. As he paused, she stepped back into the shadow against the wall, dulling the shine of her red hair. Then she spoke, in a strange low voice.

"Yes, she should be sent down," she droned. "At least she should be sent out. Two o'clock to five o'clock, is that not right? Best check your watch."

The vice-master seemed bewildered. He looked at Annie, but seemed not to see there what he wanted. He wiped his forehead with a large silk handkerchief and drew from his waistcoat a large gold pocket watch on its long gold chain. "Yes, two o'clock to five o'clock, that is the rule. It's not yet eleven..." He had fallen into a low mutter, staring at the dial; his voice now sounded like hers, or, rather, somehow, however uncannily, she had produced his own inner voice for him.

"That is right," Annie went on, echoing the mutter. "Two o'clock to five o'clock, that is clear. Now where is that red-haired woman? She came in here—she must have gone out again. Wait! Is that she?" And she pointed quickly down the shadowy corridor.

The vice-master roused himself and turned about. With a sigh he heaved his bulk into motion and lumbered off down the corridor, half calling and half muttering to himself: "Two o'clock to five o'clock, that is the rule! Two o'clock to five..."

Yet the vice-master was not alone in his amazement. For I had turned with him to follow Annie Besant's pointing finger, and caught a glimpse of a red-haired shadow, feminine in form, swiftly receding in the distance.

I turned back to the real Annie Besant standing beside us—but she was gone as well. Holmes only smiled and gestured at the alley gate opposite the direction in which the vice-master had run.

"Holmes!" I cried. "Did you see that?"

"I did not see what you saw," said Holmes, "but I perceived how you were looking, and I infer what is going on in your mind. Enough, Watson. Ladies, such as they are, can be magic enough. I do not know whether to count Russell fortunate or otherwise to have this one looking after him."

CHAPTER 5

Alice's Wonderland Garden

Most curious," I remarked.

"Curiouser and curiouser," said Sherlock Holmes. "And I daresay there is more to come."

We were strolling down the backs of the colleges, across the river Cam. Alongside the narrow lane, the Fellows' gardens lay behind green hedges and quaintly fashioned gates and walls. It was a lovely spring afternoon. Puffy white clouds lounged slowly across the blue sky. A faint warm breeze blew in our faces.

"Observe, Watson," he went on. "Russell is quite perfect, too perfect, perhaps, even to being the shy lover. There is something beneath the surface here."

"Do you think Russell is not telling us all he knows?"

"The hypothesis cannot be disregarded. Yet I should think in some other directions just now. The influences that are agitating Wittgenstein: what is their source? Russell has discounted the intellectual priorities angle, and the personal enmity angle. Yet there may be some other sources of warfare among intellectuals. Wittgenstein is not much concerned that someone will independently arrive at his ideas. He regards himself, and I take it rightly so, as far ahead of the pack. Might he not be worried that someone will steal his ideas?"

"Little good it would do the thief, though, for when he published the ideas, Wittgenstein could justly accuse him of the theft. He apparently has reliable witnesses to his priority."

"Yes, that could be so, unless the thief published them abroad. Then a priority dispute might go on for centuries, without diminishing the reputation of the first to put them in print."

"Dastardly!" I cried. "Is there not more honor among intellectuals?"

"I scarcely know of a realm in which there is less," said Holmes wryly. "Because they deal with very abstract and impersonal ideas, they refuse to admit there is any personal advantage in having them. But intellectual theft is not the only possibility in this case. It may be that there are persons who do not wish Wittgenstein's ideas to be published at all."

"You mean the conservatives whose ideas would be made antiquated by his?"

"Perhaps, or rival revolutionaries, who would not like to see the limelight switched from their subjects to his. It would be much simpler, instead of stealing his ideas, to prevent them from appearing at all."

"Indeed, Holmes! That would involve real physical threats against the man."

"Physical threats, or psychic ones. And of course there is a third influence that includes both of these."

"How do you mean?"

"I mean chemical ones, Watson—drugs. Wittgenstein's behavior may be purely a physiological reaction. The pains of throwing off an opiate addiction, and the delusions of persecution that accompany it, are all too familiar, as you may recall.* But let us consider whether there may not be an actual threat involved. If so, we do not yet know by whom such a threat would be made, or for what motive. We have assumed only intellectual issues are at stake. It may be a personal matter, carried over from abroad. I

---

* Holmes is referring to his own onetime addiction and cure, reported a few years ago in a newly discovered manuscript. Yet the symptoms described in the published account, although described as characteristics of cocaine addiction, are most peculiar: notably because cocaine is not addictive and does not cause withdrawal symptoms or hallucinations.** These are, rather, the symptoms of opiate addiction. Now, *The Sign of the Four* does depict Holmes as using

have found this to be so in most of my cases. And then there is also the Aryan question."

"The Aryan question, Holmes?"

"Anti-Semitism, Watson. It is much in vogue on the Continent just now. I detect something in the name of this Viennese philosopher, and I recall that Vienna is a city with a large Jewish population and also a center of anti-Semitism. It is possible that an enemy has dogged Wittgenstein's steps from home. Or it may be that the current international situation has brought out attacks here in England against any visitor from the German nations."

We walked in silence for some minutes. Nearby an undergraduate in a straw boater hat was lounging in the stern of a narrow flat-bottomed punt, poling the craft between the narrow banks of the Cam. Willow trees hung languidly over the glassy surface of the slow-moving stream. Hump-backed stone bridges spanned the water at intervals, and little canals meandered off to the side through the low grassy meadow. In the distance rose the Gothic spires and towers of the colleges, and the air carried the warbling of birds and the bright tones of far-off bells.

Holmes broke his silence at last. "Remarkable, is it not, Watson? We do not know if this be the land of truth, or the land of illusion. These harried philosophers, these fashionable students, and this fairy-tale land, replete with buildings from the sixteenth century. And these gardens, private to the Fellows of each college. Let us try this one. It was in a garden such as this that the paradoxical logician, C. L. Dodgson, wrote his fanciful books, and disguised himself under the alias of Lewis Carroll."

morphine as well as cocaine, and in "The Man with the Twisted Lip" Watson encounters Holmes in an opium den, whereupon Holmes jokingly asks Watson whether he will berate him for opium-smoking. It seems more than likely, then, that Holmes's addiction (if any), was to an opiate, and that this fact was disguised in the aforementioned publication. Whether this was done in the manuscript itself, or at the hands of the editor, for reasons best known to himself, is yet to be determined. It is a mystery worthy of Sherlock Holmes himself, if he is still alive.—Ed.

** The actual dangers of cocaine lie in another direction, mentioned below in Chapter 19.—Ed.

We climbed over a stile and into the prettiest garden I had ever seen. Soft green lawns curved away between curiously shaped hedges. There were long beds of roses and tulips, great clumps of tiger lilies and yellow daffodils planted in swirling patterns, and little groves of cherry trees. Fragrance succeeded fragrance in the fresh warm air as we wandered slowly into the colorful labyrinth. One lawn was set up for a game of croquet, and I should not have been surprised to see flamingos bow their heads to serve as mallets, or to have encountered the knave of hearts with his stolen tarts or met a caterpillar that talked.

"The Apostles!" Holmes mused, regaining his train of thought. "Can that be our key? This exclusive society of the intellectual elite, with its rituals and secret curses, its atheism and its strange new propensities. Yes, I believe we must look further into the Apostles."

"Unfortunately we have no list of members, save Russell himself, and those he mentioned, Keynes and Strachey. But Lytton Strachey has gone down from Cambridge, and now frequents, so I hear, a rather oddly behaved group in London known as the Bloomsbury circle. And John Maynard Keynes, I understand, is busy mainly with financial matters at the Treasury."

"You forget Whitehead. He is here at Trinity. And it should not prove too difficult to discover the other members, since we know the grounds on which they are selected. This may give us quite a useful working list for our investigations of the Wittgenstein matter. But we have a double reason to be interested in Whitehead—the strain between him and Russell. Let us see if we can locate him. Hullo, what's this?"

A white body was hunched over in the path before us, its head and arms lost beneath a large bush of white roses. It was not dead, for it twitched and made low groans and mumbling noises. Presently it scurried awkwardly backward, and a ruddy-faced man pulled himself to his feet, picking rose-thorns from his sleeves. He was dressed in sporting flannels and white cap with a brim in front, and carried a cricket bat in one hand.

"Bloody white roses!" he said, examining a small smear of blood upon his thumb. "They might as well be painted red. Oh, dear, oh, dear. Wherever have I put them?"

"Wherever have you put what?" said Holmes.

"My cricket gloves. There's a match due to begin, and I can't find them. I'm late, I'm late!"

And he began to scurry from hedge to hedge, bending down on all fours and poking about with his bat. We wandered along behind him.

"Perhaps a more orderly search would turn them up," said Holmes. "You may have time before your match. At what time does it begin?"

"I have no idea what time it begins," said the ruddy-faced man, looking up from behind a bed of geraniums. "I abhor clocks. But it is any time now. I'm late, I'm late."

He scurried across the lawn, stepping deftly around an arrangement of croquet wickets, and began poking agitatedly under a raspberry bush.

"Are you sure you have not just stepped through the looking glass?" said Holmes, in a state of rare amusement.

"Looking glass? I abhor looking glasses. They reflect only the surface of things. Where is that confounded glove?" He leaped to his feet, and disappeared rapidly around the double curve of a hedge. Holmes, tiring of the game, made no effort to follow.

"Curious, indeed," Holmes murmured. And he wandered up another green alley, apparently lost in contemplation.

Above the green hedge, a head seemed suspended in space, its eyes following us coolly, unblinking. They were eyes of the palest blue, set in a face of pale pink skin, without the slightest wrinkle or blemish. The hair was flaxen, parted in the middle, and the mouth was curved in the faintest hint of a smile.

"Who," it said, "are you?"

"I am Sherlock Holmes, and this is Dr. Watson. Who are you?"

"You are you," said the head. "You did not ask, who am I."

"Very well," said Holmes. "Who am I? Or perhaps I should say, who is I?"

"Not very grammatical," said the head. "But I know the answer. You are Sherlock Holmes, and that is Dr. Watson. The last part is irrelevant, to be sure."

"Let us try another tack," said Holmes. "Do you know Professor Whitehead?"

"Yes," said the head.

"Do you know where we can find him?"

"Yes," said the head. Its lips curved ever so slightly more.

"Where?" said Holmes.

"Over there," said the head. The blue eyes looked straight at us. The lips were now forming quite a grin.

"Where is there?"

"Where is where. There is there. Your question lacks meaning."

"And your answers lack utility."

"Bother utility. It is not the business of a philosopher to be useful."

"Nevertheless," said Holmes, "can you not define what your words mean?"

"They mean what they mean," said the head. Its grin reached almost from ear to ear. "They are not definable."

"Very well," said Holmes. "Which way do we go to find Whitehead?"

"This way," said the head, floating backward among the dogwood flowers. "Or that way. It hardly matters, you know. Words mean what we make them mean. The only question is who is to be master."

"We shall see," muttered Holmes. He turned abruptly into the alley to the left, and presently we came out into a little lawn, surrounded by violets and pansies, where sat a man of fifty in a wrought-iron chair painted in white enamel. He was writing furiously in a notebook upon a wrought-iron white enameled table, upon which sat a teapot and a broken cup.

"Professor Whitehead, I presume?" said Holmes.

The man did not look up. He was filling the page with mathematical symbols. He reached the bottom of the page, turned to the next, and began to write mathematical symbols at the top.

"I say," said Holmes, standing directly before him. "Are you Professor Whitehead? We have come on a matter of extreme importance."

The page was halfway filled with mathematics now. Whitehead did not look up or give any sign that he had noticed our presence. Presently the page was filled, and then another, and Whitehead was beginning at the top of the next.

With a shrug, Holmes gestured for us to retreat into an adjoining row of hedges.

"What cheek!" I declared. "Professor or not, I should think that common decency..."

"Aha!" came a voice on the path ahead, and the white-clad cricketeer crawled triumphantly from under a lilac bush. His flannels were speckled with lavender, and in his hand were his cricket gloves. "You see, I have found them. Pluck and determination you know, and all that rot. Now where was I?"

"You thought you might be late for a cricket match," said Holmes.

"So I was. So I was. Yet one good turn deserves another. In what can I help you, gentlemen?"

"You might tell us who is the owner of that head that has been peeping at us from behind yonder hedge."

"That?" said the cricketeer, swinging about. True enough, the head, grin and all, was staring down at us from across the way. "That's G. E. Moore, the philosopher. I'm G. H. Hardy, the mathematician. We're rather close on initials here, you see. G. E. and G. H. Too bad the family names diverge so badly, you know."

"Is he a reliable man?" said Holmes. The head had floated away again. "I mean, in ordinary matters of fact."

"Moore?" said Hardy. "He is the most reliable man in the world. He has the truthfulness of an angel. It is rather disconcerting at times. His truthfulness is proverbial. I once asked him, 'Moore, do you always tell the truth?' 'No,' said he. But I believe this is the only lie he has ever told."

"Do you think we might have a word with him?" said Holmes. "That is, if we can catch him."

"Oh," said Hardy, "he is always playing like that." He waved his cricket bat in the air and let out a shout. "Moore! I say, come out! There are some gentlemen here to see you."

Moore floated into view around the lilac bush. The grin had shrunk back to the faintest smile.

"I'm preoccupied," he said. "I must lecture to the Royal Society tomorrow, and I can't get it right."

"Don't worry," said Hardy. "I'm sure they'll like it."

"If they do, they'll be *wrong*," said Moore, pouting like a child.

"One moment," said Holmes. "You regard philosophy as important, do you not?"

"Yes, very important."

"Who is the most important philosopher now at Cambridge?"

"I am."

"Is it important for you to be the most important?"

Moore began to grin again. "Important is important. Obviously."

"What can you tell me about the Apostles?"

"Nothing," said Moore, grinning from ear to ear.

"For reasons of secrecy?"

Moore merely pursed his lips.

"Supposing I were to prove that a great danger is afoot, and that it concerns the Apostles. What would you say then?"

"Prove? You cannot *prove* that this is a lilac bush. Though it doesn't matter, you see, as long as we agree that it is."

"Would you listen to some evidence?" said Holmes.

"What good would that do?" Moore purred excitedly. "For who can prove that proof itself is a warrant of truth? We agree that the laws of evidence are true, and hence we accept what is proved by their means. But the proof is satisfactory only if we are already agreed it is a warrant of truth. Yet we cannot prove we are right in being so agreed."

"Come now," I interjected. "We *know* what is right and wrong. There is no doubtfulness about it whatever."

"Oh!" said Moore, shaking his head violently from side to side, and boggling his eyes, so that I began to feel that either *he* was mad, or *I* was mad myself. "Can you really believe *that*? You cannot *prove*, let us say, that murder is wrong, you know."

"Of course it is wrong," I declared. "If it were accepted, the human race would perish."

"Very likely," said Moore. "But that does not prove it is wrong. You would first have to prove that the contention of pessimism is wrong, that the existence of life as a whole is evil."

"Even so," said Holmes, "unless you can convince everyone that murder is right, only a few will practice it, and hence the human race will survive. Thus there is no hope of exterminating the human race, and murder would not be a good, even for a pessimist. It is only your opinion."

"Aha!" said Moore. "I did not say it was my opinion, but only that it cannot be proven that murder is wrong. It may well be wrong. It is of no interest to me in itself, you understand."

"Can we return to the matter at hand?" said Holmes. "There are certain facts that are true, whatever we may think about them."

"We often confuse what is true with what we think is true," said Moore, "and this is true. But though I cannot distinguish *what* is true from *what* I think is true, I can always distinguish what I mean by saying *that* it is true from what I mean by saying *that* I think so. After all, I understand the meaning of the supposition that what I think is true may nevertheless be false. When, therefore, I assert that it is true I mean to assert something different from the fact that I think so. Don't you agree?"*

"You are evasive," said Holmes. "Have you something to hide?"

"Do you doubt me?" said Moore. "Very well. I am lying. I always lie. Now am I telling the truth?"

Holmes did not answer.

"Stumped, aren't you?" said Moore, triumphantly. "If you believe me, you cannot believe me. And if you do not believe me, you believe me. Can you escape?"

"Yes," said Holmes. "We can leave this garden."

"Provided you can find your way out," said Moore. He had retreated back behind the hedge, and then into the branches of a nearby tree, and presently even the grin faded from sight behind the leaves.

"Silly devil, isn't he?" said Hardy. "He thinks he is a great genius, and I suppose he is. But I can show you a greater. My own friend, newly arrived from abroad. He does not like much company, but I can show you where he is."

"I should like very much to see him," said Holmes.

---

* Moore follows rather closely his own line of argument printed in *Principia Ethica* (Cambridge University Press, 1903).—Ed.

But Hardy was already on his way. Briskly we marched through the garden, around the flower beds, over the croquet wickets, across some stiles, past Whitehead who sat still writing in his notebook, through the gates and narrow alleys and Gothic archways. Hardy chattered all the way.

"Where was I? Oh, yes, cricket. A wonderful game, you know. Surprising that we stuffy British should invent a game so ripping. American baseball is the only thing to match it. You're not Americans, are you? I love America, and especially baseball. Have you come to Cambridge for a tour? You shall see our intellectual eminence here, that is clear. Would you like to learn to write like a Cambridge philosopher? There are certain simple rules. The first is, never use 'and' except at the beginning of a sentence. And the second is, put a comma every four words. But here we are."

We had arrived at another courtyard of Trinity College, one of the smaller and more secluded. Hardy led us up a flight of stairs and into a room that contained one of the strangest sights of this already very strange day.

"Here he is," said Hardy, "the greatest genius in Cambridge."

CHAPTER 6

Ramanujan the Great

We were in a room hung all along the walls and ceiling with brightly colored draperies of Indian cotton. The air was full of the smell of sandalwood and other strange Oriental fragrances. Cushions and papers were strewn in disorder about the floor. A brazier of brass burned in one corner. Near it was an idol, shining gilt in the subdued light. It was a naked woman, dancing on six legs and gesturing languidly with her six arms. There was a row of skulls about her waist, and her breasts and sexual organs were made of protruding jewels. Little heaps of fruits and candies were piled up in offering before the idol. It dominated the room like an obscene spider.

Just opposite, a short, squat man sat cross-legged on a low dais. He had the swarthy Dravidian complexion of southern India, and wore a white wrap of dubious cleanliness. His face was not quite young, but had the childish naivete of expression characteristic of his race. His long black hair was slicked down upon his skull. His limbs were flabby and weak, but his neck arched back and his nostrils flared with the arrogance of a Hindu pandit.

Holmes scanned the room without a word, and I was forced to break the silence myself.

"You are not Wittgenstein?"

"I am what I am," said the Indian in a reedy voice.

"You are not a German, surely."

"A German, an Aryan, an ancestry, a spirit... what is all that? I ask you."

"Allow me to introduce Srinivasa Ramanujan," said Hardy,

"my discovery from the mysterious East. He is the greatest mathematical genius of our day. Theorems of remarkable beauty come to him out of nowhere. And he is entirely self-taught. He had never heard of modern mathematics until he came here to England. Most remarkable, wouldn't you agree?"

"Mr. Hardy is too kind," said Ramanujan. "He is always very kind. Without him I could not come here. Without him I would still work in a commercial office in Madras. Mister Hardy is a great benefactor. May the goddess Kali protect him always." He bent forward and touched his head obsequiously to the floor between his knees.

Hardy shifted his weight uncomfortably and looked toward the door. "I say, old chaps, I must see about my cricket match. Perhaps it's not too late. I'm sure you'll have lots to talk about. Ask to see some of his theorems. Cheerio."

And with a wave of his gloved hand he bounded through the door, leaving us with the room and its strange-smelling idols.

Ramanujan smiled ingratiatingly. "You wish to see my algorithms, maybe? I have made some most remarkable discoveries, you will see."

He gestured toward several piles of papers and books that covered the floor near him.

"Why, yes," said Holmes, speaking for the first time. "We should be most interested. May I?" And he reached out his hand and rummaged deftly through the papers, while Ramanujan beamed down at him from the dais, like a monkey presiding over a rubbish heap.

"Remarkable," Holmes murmured, handing me a sheet of paper:

$$\int_0^\infty \frac{1 + \left(\dfrac{x}{b+1}\right)^2}{1 + \left(\dfrac{x}{a}\right)^2} \cdot \frac{1 + \left(\dfrac{x}{b+2}\right)^2}{1 + \left(\dfrac{x}{a+1}\right)^2} \dots dx$$

$$= \tfrac{1}{2}\pi^{1/2} \frac{\Gamma(a + \tfrac{1}{2})\,\Gamma(b+1)\,\Gamma(b - a + \tfrac{1}{2})}{\Gamma(a)\,\Gamma(b + \tfrac{1}{2})\,\Gamma(b - a + 1)}.$$

"And this as well:"

$$\text{If } u = \cfrac{x}{1+} \cfrac{x^5}{1+} \cfrac{x^{10}}{1+} \cfrac{x^{15}}{1+\ldots}, \quad v = \cfrac{x^{1/5}}{1+} \cfrac{x}{1+} \cfrac{x^2}{1+} \cfrac{x^3}{1+\ldots},$$

then

$$v^5 = u\,\frac{1 - 2u + 4u^2 - 3u^3 + u^4}{1 + 3u + 4u^2 + 2u^3 + u^4}.$$

He held them up for Ramanujan to see. Ramanujan beamed and bowed to the floor again. "It is pure mathematics," he sang out. "It is the highest form, as Mister Hardy says. Every result is perfect in itself. As Mister Hardy says, may it never be of any use to anyone."

"What!" I declared. "Shocking sentiment!" But I said it as low as I could, for Holmes went right on.

"Very interesting, I am sure. Are they all yours, Mr. Ramanujan?"

"Oh, yes," beamed the Indian. "They are all my discoveries."

"And this one?" said Holmes, holding up another piece of paper. It read:

$$666 = 10° = 1^{\square}\text{A}\therefore \text{A}\therefore$$

"Oh, yes," Ramanujan repeated. "They are all mine."

"These are only the theorems, of course," said Holmes. "What of the proofs? How do you know they are true?"

Ramanujan waved his hands complacently, his eyes looking off vacantly into the distance. He seemed hardly aware of the real world in front of him at all. "The proofs are there. For some of them. Proofs are not so important. I know they are true."

"But how do you know that?" said Holmes.

"They are revealed to me. I think, I ponder, I go into the depths of my mind. These theorems come to me. They are true. I know it."

"Where do they come from?" said Holmes. "Are they sent to you?"

"They come from the Void. Everything comes from there ultimately. Everything is Void. Life only seems to be something else. Life is maya, illusion. My theorems are links to something higher."

"But do they not come to you from elsewhere in the realm of multiplicity?" said Holmes. "From other spirits, perhaps?"

"Yes, no doubt," said Ramanujan. "They are the products of karma. Other lives, one might say."

"Other lives? Past, or present?"

"What does it matter? One shades into another soon enough. Who can truly know anything outside himself? Of any other man, how can we know, just now, if he is alive or dead? For ourselves, who knows when that moment will come—or is that moment not, truly, with us always?" He stared at us with piercing eyes.

"Infernal rubbish," I could not keep from muttering. But still Holmes led him on.

"Do you know the Apostles, Mr. Ramanujan?"

"The Apostles? I know little of the Christian religion, I fear. I am a worshipper of Kali, the Great Mother." He gestured to the six-legged idol.

"I see," said Holmes. "She is the goddess of death, is she not? She is worshipped in blood by the band of thuggee in south India, if I am not mistaken."

"There are many forms of worship," said Ramanujan. "One must not judge without sufficient thought. Destruction is an essential part of creation, you see. Kali is the divine Shakti, the energy that animates the dance. It is she that makes us what we are. She is our selves, and she is our karma."

"And how do you feel about the karmic forces now?" said Holmes. "Right now, and right here?"

Ramanujan shut his eyes and breathed deeply, expelling the breath in a long, slow rhythm.

"They are strong," he called out presently, in a voice that was loud and deep, seemingly not his own. "There are forces...forces in conflict..."

"Forces here in England?" said Holmes.

"Here in England," came the answer, after another pause. "The foreign and the still more foreign contend, the familiar loses its shape!"

"Can you not act? Have you no powers?"

Ramanujan opened his eyes. They had a glassy look. "Yes, I have powers," he said at last. "But others have powers, too. Perhaps that is why there is strife."

Holmes leaned closer. "To be precise: the powers of Ludwig Wittgenstein!"

Ramanujan's eyes went vacant, looking at Holmes and yet far away.

"Do you know Wittgenstein?" Holmes persisted.

"I see him far in the future, and far in the past, the wandering Jew, the eternal homeless. He has bound himself to the realm of illusion for ever... or almost forever. But what does it matter? In the end, the many fall away, the one remains."

Holmes was at his side, shaking the Indian's skinny arm. "Who is that one? Tell me!"

But Ramanujan's eyes were vacant. They stared but they did not see. He sat in his cross-legged posture, propped up by the habits of muscle and bone, unconscious to the world. He stayed in that pose, unmoving, as Hardy, bustling like a large ruddy white rabbit, burst into the room and hurried us through the door. The interview was over.

CHAPTER 7

The Economics of John Maynard Keynes

I felt an uncontrollable frustration after this last episode, and I could not keep myself from expressing it to Holmes as we strode across the court.

"A sidetrack, Holmes. A waste of time. Why did you not ask this absurd fellow Hardy whether it was Wittgenstein that he proposed to take us to see?"

Holmes, however, seemed again in good spirits. "The possibility that Hardy's genius was not Wittgenstein occurred to me at once, Watson. Think of it: from what we know of our somber Vienneše, is Hardy likely to be the sort of man he would choose as a friend? No, our visit was quite purposeful, and it achieved its purpose. I wished to see if Wittgenstein has any genuine rivals for the title of reigning genius of Trinity College, and I see that he has."

"Reigning mad genius, you mean."

"Perhaps, Watson, perhaps. But I have learned some other facts of interest as well. You noticed the third piece of paper I passed to you, did you not?"

"The one that said '666' and then some letters and triangles as well as numbers?"

"The very one. What did you make of it, Watson?"

"Very little, I confess. Mathematics is not my strong point, Holmes."

"Perhaps I can refresh your memory with this," said Holmes.

And he produced the same sheet of paper, neatly folded, from inside his shirt cuff.

$$666 = 10° = 1^{\square}\ \text{A.·. A.·.}$$

"It does look rather odd. I remember thinking so at the time."

"It is not mathematics at all," said Holmes, "at least not mathematics in the conventional sense. It is, rather, a code of some kind, bearing some resemblance to the paraphernalia of esoteric Masonry."

"Ramanujan is a Mason?" I cried. "The thought boggles the mind."

"Quite so, Watson, it is rather incongruous. The explanation, I expect, is somewhat more complex. But we need not interpret this piece of evidence by itself alone. Perhaps this will help."

And he drew from his other cuff a small emblem. It was a round piece of brass, two inches across, inscribed with a figure:

"I found it near the side of the infernal goddess Kali," Holmes went on. "Notice, Watson, that it also carries the number '666.' "

"What if Ramanujan should miss these things?" said I. "As he will, if they are at all important to him."

"He was in no condition to concern himself about them when we left," said Holmes, "and I can easily replace them later. But here. You have been to India. What do you make of it?" He handed me the emblem.

"It is entirely unfamiliar," I said at length, "although it has been thirty years since I soldiered in the Afghan fusiliers. Yet I would wager it does not have a Hindu look to it."

"Nor to me," said Holmes. "I should rather say Egyptian. But let us ponder its significance later. For the present, we shall step into the office of the college bursar. I should like to examine some records."

Holmes was for the greater part of an hour in the records room. When he reappeared, he had a neat list of names and dates, which he carefully folded into his pocket.

The clock was just tolling four as we stepped from the bursar's office into a dark archway between the Great Court of Trinity and the street. We had hardly taken a step when a ragged urchin in a tradesman's cap pressed a package into my hands. Before I could utter a word, he was gone.

"Quick, Holmes," I cried, "after him! He went that way, into the court. I'm sure of it."

"But this is the direction he came from," said Holmes, "and it might serve us to find out what has been following him so closely in the street." And he strode toward the silhouette of light that marked the end of the passageway. Following in the shadows, I looked at the package as best I could. It was about the size of a biscuit box, covered in brown paper and tied securely with a cord. There seemed to be no writing on it at all.

The light struck us suddenly as we emerged from the tunnel, and so did a mob of rudely shouting boys. Sturdy young ruffians they were, at least a dozen of them, and they set to pummeling Holmes and me with their fists. I was quickly backed against the wall beside the tunnel, doing my best to hold off my assaulters with one arm and to hold onto the package with the other.

Holmes, meanwhile, was accounting for some eight or nine of the boys, using his feet as well as his hands in an un-English but most effective manner. But even he might have got the worse of it, for fresh recruits were pouring in from the streets of the town, and Holmes and I seemed soon to become yet other victims of the eternal town-gown rivalry.

As the struggle was at its worst, many feet came running through the passageway. It was the students of Trinity, some in their white flannels, others in tweeds and even a few in top hat and evening dress, as they ran shouting to meet their foe. "Townies, townies! Kill the proctors' bulldogs!"

For a few moments there were bouts of fisticuffs all along the Trinity wall, and here and there noses were bloodied and knuckles bruised. The battle was fierce, but the numbers of the students quickly began to tell. Soon they had given a good account of themselves, and the townies were fleeing in every direction from Trinity Gate.

Miraculously, the package was still under my arm. I turned to look for Holmes. Suddenly a little townie, one of the last of the lot, seized the package and dashed off. He would have gotten away clear, if a man in a black suit and top hat had not suddenly seized him by the arm. Quick as a flash the man had the package in his pocket and thrust the young hoodlum from the kerb. Then he turned back toward the college.

He had an ironic mouth and a close-clipped toothbrush moustache that spread rather widely across his face and gave him a somewhat sinister look. Across his vest ran a shiny gold chain.

"I beg your pardon," said Holmes. "You are Keynes."

"Why, yes," said the man. "How did you know?"

"I have deduced it," said Holmes. "You entered the records room just now without question or greeting from the bursar, hence it is plain that you are very familiar there, even more so than other members of the college. You dress, moreover, not in the tweeds or flannels of college, but in the vest and suit of a city banker, and you wear the top hat of a treasury official. And I watched you flip a coin to decide upon a volume of records in which to search. Putting these together, I recall John Maynard Keynes, bursar of neighboring King's College, economist, treasury consultant on monetary matters, and author of a treatise on probabilities."

"A fine piece of reasoning," said Keynes. "It suggests that you, in all probability, are Sherlock Holmes, the detective."

"That is correct."

"And that fact being established, it is almost certain that this is Dr. Watson."

"Quite certain," I said.

"Have you come to investigate our annual town-and-gown riot?" said Keynes, raising his black eyebrows. "The college swells have a special grudge, since the proctors hire these young proletarians as their assistants in enforcing college discipline. Many is the night they have captured an undergraduate violating curfew after the gates are closed."

"The undergraduates seemed uninterested enough this morning," I remarked, "when some of their own dons were being attacked for their principles."

"We are here," said Holmes, "extending our interest in philosophy. And if I may return the question, what is the purpose of your own visit to the Trinity records room?"

"I am looking through the private collection of Sir Isaac Newton's papers. Newton was himself a member of this college, some two hundred and fifty years ago, and he left many valuable chests of writings when he moved to London to become master of the mint. The writings were never published, for they concern subjects rather different than the mathematical astronomy for which he is famous. But they have considerable antiquary value. Some of them had been acquired by dealers in America, and I have been endeavoring to reassemble the collection."

"At no little cost?" said Holmes.

"There is always a financial aspect," said Keynes, with a smooth smile.

"What precisely do these papers contain?"

"They concern various occult matters. Newton was interested in ancient Hermetism and other curious philosophies. He was not the only man of intellect to lead such a double life. Newton is often regarded as the fountainhead of modern science. I should say, rather, that he was the last of the alchemists."

"Perhaps not quite the last," said Holmes. "But let me ask you of a different matter, Mr. Keynes. I observed that you went through the financial drawers of the records office as well, although you are the bursar of King's, not of Trinity."

"I have made certain investments for my fellow bursar," said Keynes. "I have done rather well on the commodities market, to the benefit of us all."

"I see you have," said Holmes, looking at his gold watch and chain. "But tell me, is it not rather reckless to gamble with college funds?"

"It is not gambling," said Keynes, "it is probabilities."

"In the long run, you are sure to get a run of bad luck."

"In the long run, we are all dead," said Keynes. "Do you have any further questions, Mr. Sherlock Holmes?"

"Perhaps you would be good enough to elucidate a point of

economics for me," said Holmes. "I understand you disagree with your fellow economists in holding that government intervention in the marketplace may be a desirable thing?"

"It may often be desirable," said Keynes, "and in any case it is commoner than we believe. The government does many things whose consequences are not usually noticed, and the economist might well profit from ferreting them out."

"He might indeed," said Holmes. "For example, what would be the consequences of the government imposing severe restrictions upon the supply of a commodity?"

"If the demand remains strong, the price is sure to rise considerably."

"And this would apply, would it not, to a commodity such as drugs, whose distribution has recently been made illegal? What would an economist like yourself say, Mr. Keynes, about the opportunities presented by such an illegal market?"

The two men stood face to face in matching postures. Their heads cocked back, they stared coolly at each other with lips set firm and eyelids narrowed. Then Keynes smiled ironically.

"A properly situated entrepreneur might stand to gain much profit from such a market. Are you thinking of entering it, Mr. Holmes?"

"I am afraid I might find it already crowded," said Holmes. "It is more interesting merely to observe these strange bedfellows, the law that makes commodities illegal, and the illegal businessman who profits from their scarcity. It gives one to wonder if there are not further connections."

"Strange bedfellows would not be considered so strange if one could see beneath the surface of things. You may find much that is strange if you stay here long at Cambridge."

"I do not doubt it. We are just on our way to visit one of your stranger citizens, Mr. Ludwig Wittgenstein."

"I should not bother just now," said Keynes. "He has been absent for some days."

"How disappointing," said Holmes. "I take it you are closely acquainted?"

"Wittgenstein is an extremely promising intellect," said Keynes, "and I make it my business to follow everything that promises a future profit for this intellectual community. Good day, Mr. Holmes."

"The package!" I cried as soon as Keynes was gone. "I had it until the end of the fight, when a ruffian took it, and now Keynes has it."

"I am quite aware of it," said Holmes. "It was a package about the size of a small biscuit box, wrapped in brown paper and tied with twine in two double granny knots."

"So you did see it, Holmes! Pray, what does it mean? Is it another strange coincidence?"

"I should rather say, Watson, that it was a delivery intended for Keynes, who left the bursar's office immediately behind us. And I would say that it is a regular delivery, for the boy said not a word and he appeared punctually as the clock struck four. In his haste he mistook you for Keynes, whom I must say you tolerably resemble."

"I should hope not," I declared. "It was quite dark in the tunnel."

"Dark enough," said Holmes, as we strolled slowly across the Great Court of Trinity, under the long tiers of windows that looked down on us from the high stone walls of the quad. Undergraduates strolled through in little knots of two or three, while others lounged on the cool green lawn, and here and there passed a Fellow wheeling a bicycle, or a servant carrying a tray of sandwiches or a bucket of champagne. In the midst of the huge court, water splashed quietly down a high three-tiered fountain that was surmounted by a royal crown of stone filigree upon eight tall stone columns.

"It is unfortunate we could not interrogate one of the attacking gang," he went on, "but they have all disappeared. Still, we have progressed, Watson. The case is beginning to simplify, as the evidence grows more complex. I think we have now met all the more important members of the Apostles."

"And they are our suspects?"

"After a fashion, Watson. It is also possible that our culprit is someone who is motivated by jealousy because he was excluded from the society. This does not explain why Wittgenstein should be his target, but perhaps he does not know that Wittgenstein refused to join. The veil of secrecy would see to that."

"But the veil of secrecy should keep him from knowing that Wittgenstein was ever invited."

"All such veils have rents in them," said Holmes. "The very existence of the society is supposed to be a secret, but it is widely known in Trinity."

"And so, we should focus on someone of suitable eminence for membership, who has not been allowed to join?"

"Exactly, Watson. It is one hypothesis, at least."

"So you must suspect Ramanujan!"

"Yes, although not on these grounds alone. You recall that he, almost alone among the members of Trinity, appears to have no knowledge of the society. He could be dissimulating, of course. But if the Apostles do not figure in the motive, Ramanujan may yet be our man. He is clearly in a position to be Wittgenstein's rival, and there seems to be some general antipathy between them on racial grounds, and perhaps on intellectual grounds as well. Ramanujan is the leading light of a very traditional form of mathematics, whereas Wittgenstein is the spearhead of a radical movement that uses the new logical philosophy for an attack on the very foundations of mathematical proof. They might heartily dislike each other on those grounds alone. Recall, Ramanujan thinks up beautiful formulae but neglects to prove them, while Wittgenstein and Russell care about nothing but rigorous proofs."

"It is beyond me, I am sure. But would they go to such extremes in their struggle for precedence?"

"The lengths to which men will go depend mainly on their resources," said Holmes. "Certainly Ramanujan would have the means to prey upon Wittgenstein's mind. A man of such nervous sensibilities could be easy game for the wiles of the mysterious East."

We passed through another narrow medieval gate, so low we had to stoop to pass, and through another dark passageway. The stones under foot were worn into grooves from centuries of passing feet. In the smaller courtyard beyond, a stately marble ballustrade curved down to a quiet green lawn. On either side were tall, cool colonnades, and on the far side the great classical hall of the library rose like a Grecian temple.

"Good," I declared. "Some light is coming through this haze at last."

"It is only a hypothesis, Watson. We must not blind ourselves to some other, equally plausible, ones. For example, there is Keynes."

"Keynes? But he does not seem attuned to matters of intellectual rivalry at all. His interests go in rather different directions."

"Precisely so, Watson. Yet we must not overlook the possibility that the motives in the case may not be intellectual ones. You must admit that Keynes's character is dubious. He is a gambler, fascinated with money and with his power to manipulate things. He appears to enjoy operating beyond the bounds of propriety, or even legality, without getting caught. I have heard of his unseemly doings at Bloomsbury, and apparently in the Apostles themselves. Just what these doings are is as yet unclear, but I suspect they involve a commodity market that is lucrative and far from respectable."

"Are you saying that the brown package contains illegal drugs?"

"Very likely. They are bound to be an attraction for the adventurous. And with the recent passage of laws prohibiting their sale,* they have greatly increased in price. This cannot fail to interest someone with Keynes's interest in money. No, I don't trust the man, Watson. He is too slippery. He may represent the younger generation well enough, but for my taste, he does not strike me as steady as the gold standard."

"So these are our two suspects, eh, Holmes? What of Moore and the others?"

"I think we may safely disregard the others we have met. Moore makes a most dubious suspect, unless he is involved in something that he believes to be a prank. Hardy I would suspect even less. He is your good bluff Englishman in modern dress. Although he does have rather great loyalty to Ramanujan, and might serve, I think unwittingly, as his agent."

"You are forgetting one other, Holmes. Perhaps the most dangerous of all."

---

* Holmes is referring to the Pharmacy Act of 1908, and the international agreements of the Shanghai Opium Conference of 1909 and The Hague Opium Convention of 1912.

"Who?"

"Whitehead."

"Whitehead? My blushes, Watson. Surely you jest."

"I am all seriousness, Holmes. A man who will not greet a guest, or even respond to a direct question, cannot be trusted in decent company. Such a man will stick at nothing."

"Ah, well," said Holmes, "let us keep our eyes on him, too. It should not prove difficult to keep track of his movements. But now that we are at Nevile's Court, let us examine the rooms of our victim, Wittgenstein."

Evening was beginning imperceptibly to settle upon the towers and gardens of Cambridge. The air was soft and warm, the serenity almost palpable. Holmes paused at the foot of the stairs and waved his hand at the high stone walls. The sunlight reflecting off the creamy reddish stone and off the high rounded windows gave a mood of stately calm.

"Is it only a coincidence, Watson, that the greatest minds in England are here at Cambridge, the richest of all the schools of the kingdom? Or that the very greatest are gathered here at Trinity, with its great cathedral halls and lavish gardens, the richest of all the colleges?"

"What are you driving at, Holmes? That there is money in this matter, and more than mere intellectual pride at stake?"

"I should not doubt it, Watson. The relations are complex, but I am sure that there is something quite material and worldly that fuels these mysterious happenings. Money and brains are connected, Watson, and perhaps power as well. Keynes is only the most obvious example of the connections. Does it quite matter who appears to be most concerned with which ends? There are strong-willed men here, dedicated to attaining the best of everything they can manage. And when they come up against one another, what may they not do to attain their ends?"

CHAPTER 8

An Unexpected Ally

But our approach to the chamber of the missing philosopher was delayed once again. A figure formed out of the shadow at the bottom of the stairwell and called to us in a low feminine voice.

"Mr. Holmes! Dr. Watson! Come this way, please."

It was Annie Besant. She pressed a warning finger to her lips, and led us through a door and down the basement steps to a little storage room. It was bolted on the outside. As Mrs. Besant drew back the bolt, the door flew open and a ragged street-boy dashed out and would have run away if Holmes had not caught him by the arm.

"I believe it is the messenger boy who handed you the brown package, Watson," said Sherlock Holmes. "We are indebted to you, Mrs. Besant."

"I felt you would like a word with him," she replied. "And I felt you would be coming to this entryway, so here we waited for you."

The boy twisted and pulled under Holmes's grip. "Where's my sixpence?" he demanded. "She said she'd give me sixpence if I came with her, and then she sent me into that closet and jammed the door on me."

"There, there," said Annie Besant. "It is all for the good."

"Here is your sixpence," said Holmes, holding a coin before the lad's face. "You shall have it, as soon as you answer some questions."

The boy's eyes flashed at the sight of the coin, and he stood by expectantly as Holmes released him from his grip.

"Now," said Holmes, "what is your name, lad?"

"Please, sir, I'm called Crackie Davidson."

"What is in that brown package you delivered this afternoon?"

"I don't know, sir, really I don't. A gentleman only asked me to deliver it to Trinity Gate."

"Have you ever done this before?"

"Yes, I've delivered it every Tuesday afternoon this last month."

"And do you know if someone else was engaged to make deliveries before that time?"

The boy shuffled his feet and looked down. "I don't know, sir. Maybe."

Holmes took a second sixpence from his pocket and held it along with the other before the boy's eyes. "Perhaps you can think harder, Crackie. Perhaps you even know the name of the other messenger?"

"Please, sir," said Crackie. "There was another boy. I think it was Andy."

"Andy who? What is his family name?"

"Andy...why, Andy Jonas, that's who. Can I have my sixpence now, sir?"

"One moment," said Holmes. "Where is this Andy Jonas? We must talk with him."

"Well, 'e's not here no longer, sir. 'E's moved away."

"Where has he gone?"

"I don't know."

"I believe I'll keep this other sixpence," said Holmes. "It's only for information of discernible truth. Do you understand, Crackie?"

The boy nodded with eyes downcast.

"Well, then," said Holmes, tossing the two coins in the air and catching them alternately with his left hand, juggler fashion. "Perhaps you can tell us now to whom you were to deliver the package every Tuesday."

"It was a gentleman waiting for me, just inside the Trinity gate."

"What does this gentleman look like?"

"A regular gent, sir. Bristly moustache, fancy top hat and watch chain. A sharp-looking swell, 'e is, sir."

"It's Keynes," I cried. "The description is unmistakable."

"So it seems," said Holmes. "But let us proceed a little further. Who gave you the package, lad?"

"Please, sir, usually it's been a man at the station. Every Tuesday at 'alf past three."

"Off the London train, is he?"

"That's right, sir. And he gets on another, straightaway."

"And what does he look like?"

"Like I say, sir, usually it's a tall man, very thin, in a black coat, with a dark face. Very ugly 'e is, sir. 'E looks like a gentleman, but it's frightful to have 'im look at you."

"And he engaged you a month ago to make these deliveries?"

"'E did, sir."

"You say it is usually this dark-faced man. Was it someone different today?"

"Yes sir, it was. A short man, very pale. I didn't know it would be a different man, but 'e came right up to me, and handed over the package. I was happy enough about the change, sir, I shouldn't want to question it."

"I must know one more thing," said Holmes. "Who was chasing you this afternoon, and why?"

"As to who it was," said the boy, "it was Binkie Morris and 'is gang. Why? I don't know. They just came after me from the Fens as I came up Trumpington Road, and I thank my legs I got here ahead of them."

"I believe we can get no more from him," said Holmes. "Unless you, Mrs. Besant, have special methods to apply?"

"Why, yes, I believe I might try." Annie Besant gave a strange smile and took the boy's unwilling hand. "Look into my eyes, Crackie. Hold still!"

"Why should I?" said Crackie. "Please, sir, give me my twelve-pence and let me go."

"He shall give it to you in another minute," said she, taking a bright new shilling and holding it before Crackie's face. "Look at this very steadily. It will soon be yours as well if only you hold very still."

The boy subsided, and she went on in a low voice.

"Now, Crackie, you must go back in your mind to when first you saw the gang chasing you this afternoon. Picture their faces getting larger...so large you can see their eyeballs. Look into their eyes. What do you see?"

"That slimy face!" cried Crackie. "It's Binkie Morris. I'll smear it with blood for 'im, I will."

"Peacefully, now," said Annie. "He cannot touch you, nor you him. Only look into his eye. What is in it?"

"A bloody peeper, it is," the boy fidgeted.

"There is an image of a man in his eye, is there not? Describe it, Crackie. It is worth a shilling."

The lad subsided, then stiffened. "It's a man, all right. It's 'im!"

"Who, Crackie? Who is it?"

"It's the man from the train...the ugly dark-faced geezer who didn't come today. 'E's turned against me!" And the lad shook himself out of his vision, made a snatch at the shilling piece and seemed ready to dash away.

But quick as he was, Holmes was quicker. He clapped one hand over Mrs. Besant's coin, and caught the boy with his other.

"Let me suggest a few more questions, Mrs. Besant." Holmes turned to the lad. "Crackie, another shilling if you look again, but you must say the truth. Think now of the other man, the one who gave you the package this afternoon. Picture his eye. What is in it?"

"Yes," said Mrs. Besant, holding her face up to the boy's. "Go into his eye. Tell us what is there."

"It...it's the other gent," murmured Crackie. "The one with the moustache, who meets me at Trinity gate."

"Keynes!" I declared.

"Please, Watson," said Holmes sharply. "One more picture, Crackie. Look at the dark-faced man as he appeared last time you saw him. What is in his eye?"

"It's ugly," said Crackie. "Ugly and cruel!"

"It is worth a shiny new shilling," said Holmes. "Four shillings in all. Tell us what you see, and you are done."

The boy strained, his face quivering. "His eyes are dark," he murmured.

"And inside them?" said Mrs. Besant smoothly, in her low voice.

"Inside them... inside them..." muttered the boy, "it's dark inside there too. There's nothing. Please, sir, let me go!"

"I believe he is telling the truth," said Mrs. Besant. "I could see his other visions, but this one is as he says, nothing but an impenetrable darkness."

"I believe it too," said Holmes. And he dismissed young Crackie Davidson with a fist full of coins. For all that, the child was eager enough to get away.

Annie Besant, however, seemed inclined to linger. "I am happy to have been of service to you, Mr. Holmes. I perceive you had an altercation with the boys who were chasing this one. What does it mean?"

"It means a delivery," said Holmes, "made with some regularity to Professor Keynes. Recently it was carried out by this boy; earlier, I think, by someone else, but he does not know whom. From which I surmise that the delivery was started perhaps two months ago, but by outsiders, and only in the last month has it achieved sufficient regularity that it might be entrusted to a local messenger. Just this week, however, there has been a change in the commercial network. The deliveries are still being made, but from a different source. All we know is that previously Keynes received his packages through a dark-faced man who came up by the London train, and behind him, from someone veiled in darkness. Now the circle seems to close around Keynes and his new helper alone."

"But what can that mean?" I declared. "It is baffling, even if we take seriously all these misty visions. And what of the attack this afternoon?"

"Elementary," returned Holmes. "It is quite simply a case of commercial competition. Keynes was once involved in business with the dark-faced man and his master, but they had a falling out, and Keynes has made himself autonomous. This was not satisfactory to his former partners, who had, incidentally, rather good intelligence of his doings, and who arranged to intervene with force. It is not so different from the principle of prices that Keynes himself explained to us not long ago."

"Remarkable," I declared. "If only we knew who this dark man is, or what stands behind him. That may be the key to this entire mystery, from Russell's premonitions onward."

"Perhaps I can help," said Mrs. Besant. "I feel you have much need of me."

"You have helped us substantially already," said Holmes. "But now I think we must move swiftly."

"Think, Mr. Holmes," she said, reaching out to him vigorously, "Who can better know the identity of the dark-faced man's superior than Keynes himself?" For I intuit that the dark man is no more than an accomplice. You have last seen Keynes yourself. Come in with me, Mr. Holmes." Here she indicated the room where she had trapped Crackie Davidson, "and I shall put you into a trance, in which you shall tell me what lies deep in his eyes."

Holmes hesitated, and she took his arm and went on. "I feel that forces are moving between us already, dear Mr. Holmes. I am sure our séance together would be a fruitful one. I feel, though, that Dr. Watson does not share in this field of forces just now. I am sure he would not mind staying outside while we retire into this room, to plumb the depths together?"

And she smiled at me winningly. But Holmes pulled away.

"I appreciate your offer, Mrs. Besant," he said stiffly, "but I cannot linger with you any longer. I think it best that we investigate Wittgenstein's rooms, and as soon as possible. Good day."

And without a backward glance, Holmes hurried up the stairs, leaving me to scramble after him, and to wonder if his haste was more motivated by what lay before us, or behind.

CHAPTER 9

The Missing Philosopher Returns

udwig Wittgenstein's rooms were completely bare. There was not a decoration on the walls, nor a carpet on the floor. The bedroom was empty save for a cot, and the sitting room offered no comforts beyond a pair of canvas chairs and a card table. In the middle of the room sat a wood-burning stove, and against one wall was a metal safe.

"Remarkable," murmured Holmes. "I think, Watson, that we shall soon have some answers to the mysteries surrounding this strange philosopher and his circle of friends." He approached the safe and began to twirl the dials.

"Do you mean to burgle the safe?" I asked, with apprehension, both to its moral propriety and to the danger of being discovered in the midst of Wittgenstein's sitting room rifling through his prized possessions.

"I have already done so." The door of the safe swung open, and Holmes was now briskly leafing through the piles of papers that made up its contents. "One must never let any obstacle stand in the way of access to the facts, Watson. They are our one sure guide to truth. But hullo, what's this?"

Holmes pulled from behind the papers a small package, neatly wrapped in brown paper and tied with a string. His fingers explored the knots, and doubtless would have opened them, had not his glance, like mine, been caught by the gleam of dark metal in the depths of the safe.

It was a revolver. Holmes extracted it from the papers at the back, held its barrel to his nose, then examined the cylinders.

"Fully loaded," noted Holmes. "It has not been discharged recently. In fact, it has never been discharged at all. The blueing on the hammer is not so much as nicked, and the action is still stiff. It is quite new, and by my estimation, of comparatively recent date of purchase."

But his investigations in this direction were cut short. With a deft movement, Holmes replaced revolver and brown package in the safe, shut the door, and assumed a nonchalant position in the middle of the room. I did my best to imitate him. Within a second came a dull scraping in the hallway outside, and the door opened.

Into the room walked a dustman. He was stooped and he walked slowly, in strange fits and starts. On his head was a workman's cap, and he wore a leather jacket, a flannel shirt open at the neck, and dingy trousers and shoes. He appeared to take no notice of us, but shuffled across the room to a chair.

"Mr. Wittgenstein, I presume?" said Holmes cheerily.

The man's face contorted strangely. His lips moved, as if he were talking, but no sounds came out. His hands gestured undecidedly. There seemed to be a struggle to say something. After half a minute, his eyes suddenly focused on us. They had the most intense glow I have ever seen.

"Personal references are of no interest. Except of course for a theory of personal references. And here the problem is..."

His voice, high and resonant, trailed off, the eyes looked away into space, and his face contorted once again into its unseen dialogue.

Reflecting to myself that for all social purposes we were as good as alone, I turned to Holmes. "How did you know that this was Wittgenstein and not a dustman?"

"Elementary," said Holmes. "His clothes are perfectly clean. And despite the stoop, he is nevertheless a young man, bent over not from age or toil, but from mental exertion, and if I judge correctly, from some additional emotional agitation."

Wittgenstein stirred with annoyance. "Make your remarks pertinent to the matters at hand," he broke out. He had doffed the cap, and I could see an unruly shock of curly brown hair and a strikingly beautiful aquiline profile. He was a thin man of medium height, with fair skin and a very lean, handsome face. But his eyebrows knit in a frown, and his deep-set eyes blazed with emotion. "I make myself available out of duty to the philosophical community, but I tolerate only *serious* discussion."

"We are not philosophers," returned Holmes, "but detectives."

For the first time Wittgenstein brightened toward us. "You are detectives," he repeated. "Why do you come here? What is the mystery?"

"You are the mystery," said Holmes, "or at least part of it."

"Those are two very different propositions. Both of them true, I do not doubt. But to me, it is a far greater mystery, not why things should be the way they are, but why anything should exist in the first place instead of nothing at all."

"I am Sherlock Holmes, and this is Dr. Watson."

"Indeed?" cried Wittgenstein, almost rising from his chair. "I love detective stories. They are much preferable to philosophical literature. From that one can scarcely learn a thing. From detective stories at least one occasionally discovers something. And so I am very happy to meet you, Mr. Sherlock Holmes. I had always wished to meet a fictional detective." He bowed, German-style, from the waist, and then turned to me. "But your stories, Dr. Watson, are not of the best."

"I am sure Dr. Watson appreciates your sincerity," said Holmes. "Personally, I do not see any value in reading works of fiction at all, least of all detective novels. But since I am here, allow me to ask you a few questions."

"By all means," said Wittgenstein, leaning forward with a look of boyish pleasure.

"Why did you give away your money?"

"My money? How do you know of that?"

"Your spare furnishings speak for themselves. You have no money. And yet there are no poor men at Cambridge. Even the few struggling on inadequate means to live decently among the sons of the gentry will furnish their rooms more solidly. No, the room speaks not of simple poverty. Only a man of deep moral urges would enjoy this austerity. And only the very rich can care so little about their money to give it all away."

"You are right," said Wittgenstein. "I inherited a considerable sum from my father,* who died in Vienna not long ago. I immediately gave it away. I wish to have no false friends, such as those whom one acquires with money."

"Ah, yes," said Holmes. "And the safe?"

"It contains my papers."

"Are you afraid that they will be stolen?"

"Fire," said Wittgenstein hotly. "I am afraid that they might be burned."

"So you do care for some property, your ideas. Do you not also fear that someone might steal them?"

"Steal them? I give them away. They are not secret. I lecture here, in these very rooms, Thursday evenings from five o'clock until seven, to whoever wishes to listen. I ask only that my students be *serious*. One must attend continuously, not just once or twice. And one must arrive here on time. One must concentrate on the subject matter. For those who do, my ideas are open."

"So you do not care if one of your listeners publishes your ideas?"

"It is a matter of indifference what happens to my works," declared Wittgenstein. "I would readily consent to have all my manuscripts destroyed, if only I were sure that the works of my students and disciples were destroyed as well."

"You are not concerned about your name, then?"

"Let me tell you a story, Mr. Holmes. I once conversed at length with a philosopher. I held nothing back, I told him my deepest and truest thoughts, just as I do with everyone who asks. Afterward, he wrote an article in which he mentioned our conversation, but attributed my ideas to himself. I wrote to him and questioned his behavior. But before I received his reply, I had the news: he was dead. He had been assassinated."

"Murdered?" said Holmes. "By whom?"

"It took place in Vienna. My correspondent, like myself, was a Jew, and there are strong feelings against us in some places. What

---

* Quite right. Ludwig Wittgenstein's father, Karl Wittgenstein, was a self-made millionaire, the leading figure in the steel industry in the Austro-Hungarian Empire. He was, in fact, the Austrian equivalent of the German Krupp.—Ed.

does it matter? He is dead. It was a shock to me. It revealed that there is more than one way to receive an answer to a question."

"But here in Cambridge, is there no one whom you fear?"

"Here?" said Wittgenstein, as if the idea had only then occurred to him. He looked around the room intensely. His eyes shone.

"What do you think of Bertrand Russell?" asked Holmes.

"Russell? He is bright, very bright. And he is my friend. He has no need to steal anything of anyone."

"And Moore?"

"Moore? He is a child. A very deep child, a very good child, but a child nevertheless. He is good, but he is not generous. He could take something without batting an eye."

"Do you know Keynes, the economist?"

"Yes, certainly. He is always offering to give me things."

"What kinds of things?"

"Money and so forth." Wittgenstein waved his hand vaguely, with a look of distaste.

"And Ramanujan, the mathematician?"

Wittgenstein said nothing. He appeared to have sunk back into his inner trance.

"I believe you know Ramanujan," said Holmes. "Have you no fears regarding him?"

Wittgenstein stirred uneasily. "Whereof one cannot speak, thereof one must keep silent."

"Then let me come to the point, Mr. Wittgenstein. Russell has called us in concerning a situation that he believes is full of danger, for you and for the future of philosophy. Do you feel any disturbing influences here in recent days? Are there dangers about?"

"A danger," said Wittgenstein, "is not something that is the case. It is something that perhaps may become the case. It is not a fact. It cannot be verified."

"How, then," said Holmes, "does one verify anything of this sort? Do you prefer to wait until the danger has manifested itself, and the consequences have been suffered?"

Before Wittgenstein could answer, there came a sound of steps running up the stairs. Then the door crashed open, and Russell rushed into the room. His stiff white collar was in disarray, and he seemed to be in a state of great agitation.

"Holmes, come quickly! Ramanujan is dead!"

Russell dashed back out the door, and Holmes and I leaped to our feet. But Wittgenstein had not moved from his chair. His face twitched with intense concentration, and his mouth opened. He was attempting to speak.

"How do you verify anything?" he repeated. "How do you know if something is true or false? I know you are in a hurry to see the body, Mr. Holmes, so I will give you a *brief* answer. Suppose it is the business of a policeman to collect certain information from the people who live in his district. He writes down their names, their occupations, ages, and so on.

"But suppose he comes across a man who has no occupation. What does the policeman do? Of course, he writes *that* down too, because even to know *nothing* about a case is also useful information."

The profundity of the man struck me like the dull clap of a muffled bell. He had now lapsed back into his animated trance, and paid us not even a glance as Holmes and I rushed through the door and down into the Cambridge twilight.

CHAPTER 10

The Stroke of Death

Worse luck!" cried Holmes as we strode through the archways of the college.

"Yes, that poor devil," I replied. "I am ashamed I rallied him so. And he has taken his secrets to the grave with him."

"Not the Indian, Watson. The brown package! If only I had a few seconds more to look into it, the deepest part of this case might be plain."

A little crowd was gathered in Ramanujan's rooms. Hardy was bounding back and forth in a state of great agitation. In his excitement, he appeared to have forgotten that he grasped his cricket bat in one hand. The other men ducked uneasily this way and that as he passed.

Ramanujan's body was slumped over upon the dais. The eyes were staring, and the face was twisted into a grimace of terror.

I stepped forward and examined the body. It was still warm and pliable.

"He has not been dead as much as half an hour," I declared. "There is no sign of violence, no mark of a struggle. And there are no foreign substances upon his lips or tongue. I can see no unusual signs at all, save one, and that scarcely bears mentioning."

"You mean the horrible grimace?" said Russell. "He appears almost to have been frightened to death."

"No, not that," said I. "Something rather more medical. But let it pass."

"Come, Watson, out with it," cried Holmes. "What are you holding back?"

"His abdomen is exceedingly taut."

"And the significance of this fact? Does it mean poison?"

"No. It means constipation."

"Indeed," said Holmes. "Of what duration?"

"Really, Holmes. I should say he has been in this condition upward of three weeks."

"Can that be the cause of death?"

"I have never heard of such a thing. No, I am sure it is not."

"Our British food," said Keynes, "is not unjustly criticized for its indigestibility."

"It is this infernal British weather," declared Hardy. "We live here upon a foggy rock. The man has been pining away since he arrived. I told him he should be happier in a sweeter land like Norway, or America."

"Ah, death," said Whitehead. "Ah, death. Never glad confident morning again. Still, he should never have come here. England is suitable only for the English."

"Rampant bigotry," cried Hardy. "That is just such an attitude as is now leading us into a disastrous war."

"Have you no love of motherland?" returned Whitehead. "It is the Bosch, and not we ourselves, who are preparing a war of aggression. I fear Russell has swayed your opinions with his brittle eloquence."

"I fear that Hardy is the only one I have convinced," said Russell. "We may soon all of us pay the price of your sentimental patriotism."

Through all this, only Moore stood aloof. His unblemished face was clouded, and he looked as if he might burst into tears.

"It is an unprofitable discussion," said Keynes. "Come what may, we shall have to find means to pay for it. But let us for the moment consider how we must deal with our present difficulties." And he waved his hand in the direction of the body.

"Quite right," said Hardy. "It is foul play. Who could have done it?" He looked very menacing with his bat.

"Did Ramanujan have enemies?" said Russell.

"There was bad blood between him and your man

Wittgenstein," declared Whitehead. "One foreigner against another, and on British soil. We are continuously being called in to
set matters right."

"Where is Wittgenstein just now?" put in Keynes.

"He has been gone these five days," said Russell. "But no! He
has only just returned."

"You see?" said Whitehead. "It makes a pattern, a palpable
constellation. We may call the whole a single event. The one man
with a motive against Ramanujan, the one whose actions go
unaccounted for, is the one missing at the time of the murder.
And, you will notice, he is the one who fails to come and see the
body. He will not pay his respects, even in death."

"It is not yet so clear," said Holmes, looking up from searching
through a pile of papers and old teacups. "Wittgenstein has been
with Dr. Watson and myself this past half hour. The timing is not
such as to exclude all possibility that he has been here, but it makes
it unlikely. And, furthermore, there is the question of a weapon.
The body has not been touched."

"True, true," cried Hardy. "How can it have happened?"

"Who was the first to discover the body?" said Holmes.

"Why, I was," said Hardy.

"And you were the last person in this room to see him alive,
were you not?" Holmes looked around the assembled faces.

"I suppöse so," said Hardy, leaning on his bat.

"And where were you in the last few hours, between the time
we saw you last, and the time you found the body and gave the
alarm?"

"Indeed," said Hardy. "Where was I? Why, right here. No, I
went off to find a cricket match, and I encountered Whitehead,
who invited me to take tea with him and discuss the foundations of
mathematics."

"Did you do so?" said Holmes, turning to Whitehead.

"Did I do so? This afternoon, you mean. Yes, I seem to recall, a
quiet afternoon in the garden, and a pleasant conversation over the
teacups. Light conversation and lemon tea, I recall."

"It is true," said Moore. "I saw them."

"And you, Keynes?" said Holmes.

"I paid a call upon my friend and fellow member of the Royal

Society, Mr. Bertrand Russell. We had occasion to discuss matters of politics and economics."

"I am sorry," said Moore. "It is not entirely true."

"What is not entirely true?" said Holmes.

"I do not know that it was lemon tea. Of the rest, I will testify."

"Excellent," said Holmes. "We are nearing the end of our questions. Perhaps Mr. Russell could be of assistance in identifying this."

He laid out a piece of paper containing a curious symbolism:

6.1203 . . . . I wish to examine the proposition $\sim(p.\sim p)$ (the law of contradiction) in order to determine whether it is a tautology. In our notation the form '$\sim\xi$' is written as

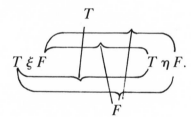

and the form '$\xi.\eta$' as

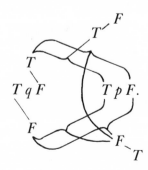

Hence the proposition $\sim(p.\sim q)$ reads as follows

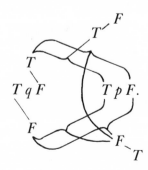

"It is Wittgenstein's truth-function," said Russell. "He regarded it as among his most important discoveries. Where did you find it?"

"Among Ramanujan's papers. It is the only one that did not fit the pattern of the rest."

"Is there nothing further here that would constitute a clue?" said Russell. "Have you completed your searches, Holmes?"

"Not quite," said Holmes. "But there remains only the bathroom." He opened the door to a small tiled room. "And there is nothing here, save for a curious bottle upon the drain. I have my doubts that it will prove to be soap."

"Indeed?" cried Hardy. "What can it be? Do tell us, Holmes."

And he wheeled about excitedly. His cricket bat, still attached to his heedless hand, swung through the air and smashed the bottle into the sink. A strange brown liquid gurgled down the drain.

"Oh, dear, oh, dear," cried Hardy. "It may have been an important clue."

"From the smell," said Holmes, "I would judge that it is some compound of sandalwood incense, perhaps connected with the worship of the goddess Kali. Let us be gone, Watson. There is nothing further to do until an inquest is made."

"An inquest?" said Keynes. "It hardly seems necessary."

"It is common procedure in the case of a murder," said Russell.

"Doubtless so," said Keynes. "But I should point out, if I may, that this appears to be a perfectly ordinary death. Ramanujan has been in poor health since arriving in England, and it is entirely appropriate that he should die of our climate and our conditions, just as many of us have succumbed to the steamy rigors of India. No, I should think any competent medical opinion would be that the death is purely natural, although of course deeply to be regretted. The probability that it is anything else is so small that we can safely disregard it. To call for an inquest would be to put this incident under a cloud, and Trinity College with it."

"It is true," said Whitehead. "We must not think only of ourselves."

"I might further point out," said Keynes, "that Ramanujan was not an English citizen. An inquest could easily reach the newspapers. It might lead to an incident being manufactured, and to questions being asked in Parliament, such as might prove embarrassing at this time when England needs all the support from her Indian colonials that she can muster. And, I might add, at a time when the University Grants Committee has asked that the salaries of the Regents Professors be increased."

"Quite right," said Whitehead. "We are letting our emotions take this incident out of all proportion."

"Gentlemen," said Holmes, "I must insist. We cannot let politics stand in the way of truth in this matter. The situation may not be conclusive, but let us have every fact we can. I appeal to you, Russell, and to your sense of fair play, Whitehead."

"Quite right," said Russell. "It must be done."

"I should hope I should ever do right," said Whitehead. "Yes, let us take the consequences."

"Very well," said Keynes. "I shall call Constable Dogberry and Dr. Doolittle, the coroner. We can count on them to be discreet. I know Doolittle well, and have had occasion to direct some investments for him on the commodities market."

"Excellent," said Whitehead. "You are a man of affairs, Keynes. We will leave the arrangements to you. All sides are satisfied. It is a most English solution."

"Quite so," said Keynes. "Now I hope you will excuse me, gentlemen. I must make arrangements about the mourning crêpes, for the world of the intellect has suffered a great loss. And I must catch the evening train up to London, for I meet in the morning with my brokers."

"Come, Watson," said Holmes. "We can be of no further use here."

"Where are we going?" said I, as we hurried outside.

"Back to Wittgenstein's rooms, Watson. We may yet close this account tonight."

The windows above the stairs in Nevile's Court were dark. "Good," murmured Holmes, "he has gone out again. We can complete our work."

The room stood bare, as before. Holmes went directly to the safe. It was the work of a few seconds to open it. The door swung back.

It was empty.

"Too late," cried Holmes. "He has disappeared again. And this time, I fear, he may not be seen in Cambridge again."

"So he is the murderer!" I cried. "To leave like this is a sure admission of guilt."

"I do not think so," said Holmes. "It may be only an admission of fear, or, better yet, an act of prudence. For I think Ramanujan and Wittgenstein were both menaced, and from the same source."

"Indeed?" said I. "What source can that be?"

"I may be able to tell you shortly. Observe, Watson."

He seated himself at the card table and drew from his sleeves and pockets a series of documents.

"These three," said Holmes, "I managed to take from the safe just before we were interrupted by Wittgenstein's untimely return."

The first was a series of short sentences, numbered from 6.5 to 7. The top lines read:

> 6.5 When the answer cannot be put into words, neither can the question be put into words.
> 6.521 The solution of the problem of life is seen in the vanishing of the problem.

"This must be the same series from which we found an excerpt in Ramanujan's rooms, Holmes. It confirms that Ramanujan was stealing his ideas. Wittgenstein must have found out about it, and killed him."

"You are right on the first point, Watson, but not on the others. Look at this."

And he indicated a second page:

$$\cfrac{1}{1+}\ \cfrac{e^{-2\pi\sqrt{5}}}{1+}\ \cfrac{e^{-4\pi\sqrt{5}}}{1+\ldots} =$$

$$\left[\frac{\sqrt{5}}{1 + \sqrt[5]{\left\{ 5\frac{3}{4}\left(\frac{\sqrt{5}-1}{2}\right)^{5/2} - 1\right\}}} - \frac{\sqrt{5}+1}{2} \right] e^{2\pi\sqrt{5}}$$

$$\int_0^\infty \frac{dx}{(1+x^2)(1+r^2x^2)(1+r^4x^2)\ldots}$$

$$= \frac{\pi}{2(1 + r + r^3 + r^6 + r^{10} + \ldots)}$$

"These are some of Ramanujan's theorems. They were stealing from each other!" I exclaimed.

"It would be more plausible, Watson, to infer that they were doing what most intellectuals do: they were exchanging copies of their work in progress."

"But they were rivals and enemies."

"Not necessarily in the extreme," said Holmes. "The intellectual world, my dear Watson, is exceedingly competitive, but its competition can take strange forms. To give someone a copy of one's work is not merely a gift, it is a challenge. It is a way of proving one's claim to priority. And hence to reciprocate with a copy of one's own work is not merely to return gift for gift, but to meet challenge with challenge. And beyond all this, there may even be some community of interest. You see, Wittgenstein was a mystic too. Look at the first page again: '6.522 There are, indeed, things that cannot be put into words. They make themselves manifest. They are what is mystical.' and Number 7: 'Whereof we cannot speak, thereof one must keep silent.' "*

---

* Wittgenstein's work in progress, of course, was his *Tractatus Logico-Philosophicus*, finally published in 1921 in German, translated into English in 1922, and reprinted in the United States by the Humanities Press Inc. in 1974. By the time it was printed Wittgenstein had repudiated its contents.—Ed.

"I say, Holmes, you are right!"

"Elementary, my dear Watson, elementary. And they may even have realized lately that they have a common enemy."

"An enemy? Who, Holmes?"

"Someone known to both of them. Look at this, Watson." He unfolded the third piece of paper:

$$666 \ = \ 10° \ = \ 1^{\square}\,\text{A}\therefore\text{A}\therefore$$
$$7° \ = \ 4^{\square}\text{G}\therefore \ \text{D}\therefore$$

"Why, it is the same as the paper you discovered in Ramanujan's room, but with an additional line."

"Yes," said Holmes. "And I believe it is connected with this emblem." He laid the two papers, Ramanujan's and Wittgenstein's, together on the table, and set the emblem before it.

"Observe, they all have an Egyptian or Masonic motif."

"Can you decipher them, Holmes?"

"I believe so, with the aid of this." And he unfolded his last paper, a list of names with dates set against them, ranging from 1890 to the present. "It is a list of students who matriculated at Trinity since Russell's early days, and who took honors in mathematics or philosophy. Some of them, I think, may have been excluded from the Apostles, despite their intellectual eminence, and hence they may feel a grudge against the charmed circle still today."

"But neither Wittgenstein nor Ramanujan is a member of the Apostles."

"Quite right, Watson. But that may be exactly what has inclined our evil genius in their favor. For I do not believe he was so much threatening them, as attempting to bring them over into his cabal."

"But how can you know this, Holmes?"

"Elementary," said he. "They both have messages and tokens from this evil genius, which they both hold as prize possessions. This leads me to believe they were gifts from a friend, and that only gradually have they come to fear their friend's influence."

"Remarkable, Holmes. It does cast a new light on the matter. But how could such an influence operate? Wittgenstein and Ramanujan were both strong-willed men, and both had good friends within the Apostles. They would not wish to destroy their friends. Nor, indeed, have they made any move to do so."

"You are right," said Holmes. "But consider the matter one step further. Both Wittgenstein and Ramanujan are interested in mysticism, and their friend is obviously an adept in some mystical cult, judging from the messages he sent them. Once he had them interested, he could begin to play upon them with psychic influences, and in conjunction with these, to sap their wills in other ways."

"How do you mean, Holmes?"

"Do you recall the sole medical peculiarity in Ramanujan's death?"

"You mean his extreme case of constipation? I cannot see what bearing it has. One does not die of tight bowels, Holmes."

"No, indeed, but we were talking of something else. Do you know of an agency that can cause such constipation?"

"I think I begin to see your drift. The newer preparations of opium tend to bring the lower digestive system to a standstill."

"Exactly, Watson. Ramanujan must have been taking strong drugs for weeks, at least."

"But no drugs were found in his room."

"Someone could have removed them. Or even more likely, Ramanujan had used up his supply, and was in a distressed state while waiting for the weekly delivery."

"That is logical, Holmes. And taking drugs would not be out of keeping with the Hindu character. But Wittgenstein seems to be another case. He is, after all, an extreme ascetic."

"And so he is. But his friend could easily have introduced them as part of his mystical rites. And once established in the bodily metabolism, they are hard to shake off. Wittgenstein, of course, was a man of strong will and great intelligence, and he apparently began to see what was happening. That would account both for his strange behavior and for his unaccountable five days' absence from Cambridge."

"Yes, and for the brown package, hidden in the back of the safe."

"Exactly, Watson. Though it cannot be taken as a good sign that Wittgenstein has disappeared, taking the brown package with him."

"He may have taken it only to dispose of it."

"Let us hope so. In the meantime, let me see what can be done to establish the identity of our villain. It is not entirely certain that he is on this list, but if I can make the code fit one of these names, it is very likely he."

With that, Holmes pulled off his coat and began to scribble upon his papers. For an hour he struggled, rising fitfully from time to time to pace the room and tear at his fingernails. I had long since learned to leave him alone at times like this, so I lounged in the stairwell, smoking a cigar and staring up at the silhouettes of the Trinity College towers.

It was ten o'clock before Holmes appeared at the door.

"Let us be off, Watson. The culprit is not here in Cambridge at all. We have only just time to catch the train."

"For where, Holmes?"

"For Chancery Lane, Watson. We are onto him now!"

"But who is he, Holmes?"

"He is a worthy antagonist indeed," said Holmes. "I should have known it earlier. He has already earned the title of the wickedest man in England."

And with these enigmatic words, he lapsed into silence, his pipe clenched between his teeth. He did not speak again until at midnight we reached the bleak outskirts of London.

PART TWO

IN DARKEST NIGHT

CHAPTER 11

The Tale of the Cabbala

Does the name Aleister Crowley mean anything to you, Watson?"

We were riding in a cab through the dark streets of London, over the cobblestones of the old medieval heart of the city.

"No, nothing," I replied. "Unless there is some connection to Crowley's Ales."

"There is indeed," said Sherlock Holmes. "Aleister Crowley is the heir to that alcoholic fortune. It appears he has adhered rather more closely to the moral tone of the source of his fortune than he has to his father's own predilections. The elder Crowley retired a rich man, and devoted himself to propagating the strict biblical faith of the Plymouth Brethren, a sect that regards orthodox Christianity as far too dissolute. And God knows, it may be. Yet devil take it, I am no theologian. Aleister Crowley came into his fortune, as sole heir, at the age of twenty-one, and proceeded to establish himself as much a paragon of evil as his father was of good. In other respects, I admit, they appear to have much in common. Both father and son have a flair for the dramatic, and regard, or regarded, themselves as members of the elect. Aleister Crowley showed this streak not long after he came up to Cambridge."

"So he was on your list, Holmes. That is how you have found him."

"Exactly so, Watson. He matriculated at Trinity College in 1895, just three years after Russell, who has been there, of course, almost continuously since that time. Crowley stayed three years, and left without taking a degree."

"Ah! That may be significant, Holmes."

"It may be, or it may not. We do not know yet under what circumstances he left. He was not sent down, and his academic record, as far as I can ascertain, was excellent. He was the president of the University Chess Club, and he specialized in mathematics, as well as, privately, in poetry."

"And so he might have acquired an emnity for Russell then."

"He may have. Crowley was bright, but I daresay not popular. He was rich and smart enough to be arrogant, and too rich and smart to be so without the proper connections. Russell, I suspect, may have represented all that Crowley lacked and disliked— Russell's social background, his membership in the intellectual elect of the Apostles, his sense of political responsibility. Russell's radicalism must have irked Crowley, the *parvenue* confronting the genuine *noblesse*. While Russell was writing of German social democracy, Crowley was attempting to pose as a member of the ancient aristocracy, buying a house on Loch Ness so he could style himself Laird of Boleskin, and writing denunciations of modernity in the manner of that German madman Nietzsche."

"It seems logical, Holmes. But one thing eludes me. How did you find the name of Aleister Crowley in that code, in that '666' and all that?"

"Have you never heard of the Cabbala, Watson?"

The light flickered through the windows of the cab as we passed from streetlamp to shadow and back again. Holmes's face, familiar though it was to me from our long years of acquaintanceship, was etched by shadows into the semblance of a sinister mask.

"I have heard of cabals and other nefarious conspiracies. No doubt this may be one, but how does that knowledge help to decipher those cryptograms?"

"Bravo, Watson. You have the correct family of words, at least. The etymology of your nefarious cabals does indeed run to the Cabbala. But it is far more ancient. It derives from a secret method developed by the Hebrews, in their time of exile, for reading secret meanings in the holy texts. This practice divided the community of believers into inner and outer groups, a feature that could not but appeal to Crowley, and all those like him who have practiced this art over the years. And of course it was useful for preserving the more mystical and apocalyptic aspects of the faith in hostile environments. The essence of the technique is a series of correspondences between numbers and the letters of the alphabet. Every word has its number, comprised by the sum of the numbers of the letters of which it is spelled. And conversely, of course, any number might be translated into a word."

"Remarkable, Holmes. But is it not possible that one number could be translated into more than one word? The method seems to admit an intolerable ambiguity."

"It does, Watson. Yet it was this interchangeability of meaning that first endeared it to the Hebrew sages. Recall, they were looking for secret messages in the books of the Old Testament. By translating a word into its number, they could discover which words were equivalent to it by virtue of having the same number. Thus were built up families of correspondences, and the meaning of each word was amplified by its relatives. This was believed to be especially significant in the case of names. Proper names were held to convey magical powers to whoever knew them and could utter them aloud. Hence one would keep secret one's own name, lest others have power over you. The name Jehovah, which the Hebrews called Jahweh—this name was one of these. For centuries it was kept secret, and then only hinted at by cryptic forms, and by reference to its Cabbalistic number. It was for revealing Jehovah's name to the entire world that Jesus was crucified by the orthodox."

"Shocking, Holmes! That these primitive peoples of ruder times should take respect for their fetishes to such extremes."

"For them it was a serious business." In the intermittent shadows, Holmes's face seemed shaped into a hideous grin, and I half felt I was being mocked by a demon. But his voice went on calmly. "As you can see, the Cabbala has not been regarded as a toy. Its adherents have felt they could use it as a means for divination and other dark arts. One might look up the words that have the same number as a person's name, and thereby foretell his future. It is for this use, and for writing cryptograms for the purposes of secret societies, that it has survived to this day.

Crowley doubtless belongs to such a society, and it was by introducing Wittgenstein and Ramanujan to the intricacies of this code that he hoped to induce them to join."

"And the '666' and so forth is Crowley's Cabbalistic name?"

"So I have discovered, Watson, but not without a good deal of trouble. I have had to translate his name first into Greek. And it may not be without significance that '666' is mentioned in the Bible, in the Book of Revelation. It is the number of the Great Beast of the Apocalypse, with its seven heads, which represents blasphemy and is ridden by the Scarlet Woman, the Whore of Babylon."

"And so this emblem with the seven-pointed star and the number 666 represents the beast also." I struck a match and examined the brass emblem once more.

"But what is the strange set of circles above?"

"Cannot you guess, Watson? I have an idea that it may fit well into Crowley's character. Notice, he is undoubtedly pleased that his name coincides with the arch-symbol of evil."

The match went out, and I hastened to strike another.

"That explains most of it, Holmes. What of the rest of the cryptogram?" And I pointed to the part that read:

$$10° = 1^\square \text{ A.}\therefore \text{ A.}\therefore$$
$$7° = 4^\square \text{ G.}\therefore \text{ D.}\therefore$$

"That is what gave me the first clue. 10° and 7° obviously mean the tenth degree and the seventh degree, suggesting rank in some organization. But what organization? One line tells us that the seventh degree is equal to the fourth level in something called G.∴

D.˙., which brings to mind the Order of the Golden Dawn, a secret society in London devoted to the occult arts, of some twenty years standing. I had heard that this society underwent much internal schism a few years ago. Hence it is not unlikely that the A.˙. A.˙. is a rival organization, which claims to be higher, as shown by the fact that Crowley claims the rank of tenth degree, with a position of number one in the A.˙. A.˙., while pointing out that the Golden Dawn only represents the seventh degree and a position of number four. Finally I recalled that the Cabbala uses the symbol of the Tree of Life, which is a diagram representing something like the seven chakras of the Hindu, except the Hebrews use ten and call them the Sephiroth. The higher one's mystical advancement, the higher the Sephiroth one reaches on the Tree of Life. Crowley is claiming that the Golden Dawn reaches only the fourth Sephiroth, while he himself has reached the first, and no doubt claims the rank attached to this, of *Ipsissimus*. But look, Watson. We are nearing our destination."

I glanced from the window. We were passing the precincts of Gray's Inn, where British barristers have had their chambers since medieval times.

"It is all very interesting, Holmes. Yet surely it has not been only from his dabbling in these pagan arts that Crowley has acquired the title of 'the wickedest man in England'?"

"You are quite right, Watson, it is not. But let me relate to you an incident that has become rather notorious. In 1905, Crowley set out to climb Kanchenjunga in the Himalayas. It is nearly the tallest peak in the world, and its ascent has not yet been accomplished. Crowley set out with five other white men, and of course with a small army of native bearers. After two months' travel, they established a forward camp within a few thousand feet of the summit. The weather was bad, however, and the party was forced to hold up in their tents for some weeks. Their food was running low, and soon the season during which the descent could be accomplished was coming to an end. At this juncture, a dispute arose among the party. Crowley, who had been the leader of the expedition, was deposed by unanimous consent of the others. The remainder of the party started down, and only Crowley stayed behind in the advance camp.

"Within half an hour after the party left camp, they were struck by an avalanche, while Crowley watched from the slopes above. He then coolly folded his tent and picked his way down across the glacier, without bothering to dig out the others or recover the bodies."

"Good heavens, Holmes! Do you mean to say that he started the avalanche?"

"No, that itself has never been supported. At least not by ordinary human means."

"You mean possibly by some inhuman means?"

"I should not care to say. I only mean this narration to illustrate the icy determination and inhuman coolness of our antagonist. He is a man of many skills and wide experience, Watson, and we shall have to be on our guard. He is said to have killed a man in Calcutta. To evade possible inquiry, he embarked on a journey with his pregnant wife through the wilds of highland Burma, cowing the primitive and violent tribes of that region, ascending the Mekong and descending into south China, thence making his way across the Pacific and back to Europe. He is said to be familiar with the occult arts of India, with the drugs and dervish dances of the Arabs, and, some aver, even with the blood sacrifices of ancient Mexico. On top of this, he has a dangerous influence over women. More than one man has lost his sweetheart, or his wife, to Crowley's wiles,* although it is a collection that Crowley hardly keeps for long. But hold, we are here."

"What do you intend to do, Holmes? Surely we cannot pay a social call on such a man, and at such a time of night. Do you hope to confront him with your evidence, and force him to admit his guilt?"

"Perhaps not," said Holmes, pulling down his deerstalker cap. "But it is just possible, in the case of an operator such as Aleister Crowley, to catch him in the act."

---

* W. Somerset Maugham depicted just such a case, thinly fictionalized, in his first novel, *The Magician*. —Ed.

CHAPTER 12

Crowley's Castle

We had arrived at a venerable house in Chancery Lane. Its slate roof made a jagged silhouette against the midnight sky, a black form upon the mist that glowed dully, as the night sky does, in any large city even in the depths of night. Behind iron grillwork some dim lights shone at the windows, despite the hour. Holmes pushed through the gate and strode up a short set of steps to a front door overhung with an enormous lintel.

Holmes looked through the keyhole, then put an ear to the door. He shook his head, descended the steps, and made his way inside the iron fence along the yard and a half of sunken pavement that serves as an exterior garden for an English town house. Here and there he examined a window, but each was protected by its grill without, and tightly curtained within. A basement door did not yield—again barred. At the rear of the house, there was a servants' entrance. But its door was of solid oak, without so much as a keyhole, and seemingly crossbolted from within.

"A fortress," murmured Holmes. "The front door is likely our best bet."

At the front door, Holmes drew a short piece of wire from his pocket and made to insert it in the keyhole. Then the door swung slowly open of its own accord. We stepped into a marble foyer, up some farther steps, and into a long corridor. Neither butler nor master was in sight.

The house was curiously arranged. The corridors of polished parquet were dimly lit by braziers and antique oil-burning lamps, and here and there by candelabra caked with drippings of wax. Room followed room in no apparent order, their walls hung with tapestries and Oriental rugs. Here a curtain of dark velvet served in place of a door; there, a set of tall lacquer screens; in yet another place, heavy oak panels that slid noiselessly aside to the touch. The atmosphere throughout was thick and yet full of strange eddies and currents: some places warm and stagnant, while in others a cool and almost chill breeze seemed to blow out of nowhere, for there were no vents to be seen, and halfway across a room, passing a gilt harpsichord or an enameled urn, the air would suddenly drop to tepid stillness. In other places, strange plants seemed to writhe in the half light.

All the downstairs rooms were empty of human life. Silently we passed from each to each, 'til Holmes came to a halt and beckoned me forward. There across an empty chamber, lit by tapers burning in opaque amber vials, was a familiar gilt statue: the six-legged dancer with her six arms pointing languidly toward every meridian, and her legs spread in an infinity of obscene poses. It was Kali, goddess of death.

We stood for a second in silent recognition. Still nothing stirred in the house, though the scents of that heavy air seeped over more insidiously upon us. There was nothing definite in the nostrils, yet I felt the hint of a ghostly sandalwood, mixed with currents of jasmine, and then a sudden billowing whiff of something like burning caramel, and almonds, and, incongruously, of alfalfa and new-mown hay. In an olfactory daze I followed Holmes through a corridor of gleaming marble and up a spiral staircase.

I do not know how long we had been in that house, nor how long it took to ascend those steps. They seemed to spread out interminably, one above the next, as I trudged dutifully after Holmes's receding figure. Time slowed almost to a halt, and my heart pounded quietly, steadily, like the beats of an ancient clock. Was it only my imagination, or did some low, ghostly laugh mock my eternal, foredoomed ascent? At last we reached the top.

I cannot say how the upper stories were furnished, nor even if we stepped off that marble landing into empty space. The sweet smells grew thicker, the air even heavier and more liquid. Cobwebs blocked the way in that dim corridor, and I wiped them fruitlessly with the back of my hand across my perspiring brow. Or were they bats, these dark shapes that swooped out of the cornices and flapped their wings across my face? And worse yet, I realized with a chill that was far more genuine than those cold whirlpools of this murky ocean: Holmes then disappeared!

Yet I had no time for panic, for I knew that I was not alone. A human figure was walking toward me in that upper chamber, and as it came within the distance of recognition, I had a shock of surprise but not of fright. It was Whitehead! With his gray hair and scholarly demeanor he was moving slowly toward me across the room.

Yet when we were closer, I saw I had been mistaken. It was not Whitehead at all, but the stiff, gracious figure of Bertrand Russell, advancing to meet me in that strange place. How could he be there? Yet it was reassuring to find a friend, when all I could expect was to meet a dangerous enemy upon his home ground.

Still Russell advanced, but more and more slowly. His stiff white collar was unmistakable. His face held a look of high abstraction. He seemed lost on some philosophical heights. And then, with a thrill of horror, I saw that he too was a phantom, for his eyes looked through mine, and mine through his, as his face softened and faded and yet another form took his place. It was something feminine, with delicate curving eyebrows and long dark hair and a cruel, sensuous mouth. She wore gleaming stones around her neck, amethysts and rubies set in gold, it seemed, and, farther down, her ample breasts and hips and the curve of her navel and her dark *mons veneris* told me that she was completely naked!

I stood stock still in that strange place, unwilling to take another step. Yet still she advanced, her face nearing mine, her breath hotter and hotter as she approached. Her jeweled arms stretched out, her phantom fingers reached toward my shoulders. The phantom was about to consume me: no, no, flashed my mind, racing ahead of my languid sensations, a hallucination is about to pass right through me and dissolve like the mist upon the head-lands of rocky, firm, old Mother England.

And then we touched.

The hands fastened upon my shoulders in a grip of steel. Real flesh and bone, they were, long skinny fingers with the strength of a Mackenzie steel trap. They tightened, and shook, and I was struggling like a rat in the mouth of a hungry terrier. My phantom had me in its grip, and I could not escape!

I screamed.

"For God's sake, Watson," came a familiar voice.

It was Holmes. He stood before me, face to face, and his hands held my shoulders and rocked me firmly to and fro. "Come to your senses, man."

The mocking laugh sounded again, but this time louder, clearer. There was no question now; it was a real human voice. It came from behind Holmes. We were no longer alone.

It laughed again, but trailing off into something like a snarl. Holmes turned, and we both beheld a tall, corpulent figure standing in the lighted doorway. It was a man, draped in a cloak, with a shaven head and shining eyes.

"You've ruined the vision, you fool," it snarled.

"The illusion, you mean," said Holmes.

"Call it what you will," said the man. "Here I am myself. I am he whom you seek, Aleister Crowley."

CHAPTER 13

The Wickedest Man in England

Crowley led us into a sitting room with a large fireplace. On the grate some embers glowed, and around the walls old-fashioned gas lamps in brass fixtures gave off a subdued light. Near the fireplace were several large leather chairs and a heavy sofa with pillows of purple and scarlet brocade. Along the walls there were heavy tables with legs carved in the shapes of gargoyles, the tabletops strewn with papers and maps and irregular piles of books with thick leather bindings. Curious, unidentifiable trinkets lay here and there in that strange disorder, and on the walls were gray silk rugs of Oriental design. The far end of the room, opposite the fireplace, was lit but dimly in the distance, and seemed to be covered by nothing but a large gray curtain.

Yet after our voyages through that house, this room held an atmosphere of unusual normalcy, and I eyed the comforts of an easy chair with uneasy longing.

Crowley stared at us imperiously. The massive dome of his shaven head, surmounting that strong, fleshly face, gave him an almost superhuman appearance, like some creature from beyond the ordinary world and its ordinary idols as well.

"A man's home is his castle," he said coldly. "If you invade it, by entering uninvited, you must be prepared to suffer the consequences."

Holmes stared back with his customary sang-froid. "I have

heard that you claim certain powers, Crowley. Do you not know what brings us here? You do seem to have been expecting us."

"It is no great feat to discern a strain in the local psychic atmosphere," said Crowley. "And as for what brings you, I could tell it well enough by the simple expedient of reading your minds, my dear Mr. Holmes. And of course Dr. Watson. Shall I show you what you seek?"

He raised his arm toward the rear of the room, his black cloak hanging down in folds like the wing of some great bird of prey. The gray had suddenly become opaque gauze, and behind it was another room. It was his laboratory, the den of a medieval alchemist complete in every archaic detail. Upon a long brick furnace sat cast-iron pots, and noxious fumes rose from them to the low, sooty ceiling. There were glass tubes rising like the coils of a distillery, with strange clear liquids bubbling and steaming through their turns and dripping down again slowly, in dire, persistent drops, into crystal vials. Upon the floor of that hellish room were bones and remains of animals, and suspended from the center of the ceiling arch was a stuffed salamander or crocodile, turning slowly this way and that upon an iron chain. In the midst of the room was a workbench, and on it were a series of glass retorts, each big enough to hold a one-year-old child. From each retort came a long glass spout tapering to a tiny point. And as I looked more closely at those glass pots, my stomach jumped into my throat—each one held a ghostly embryo, dripping a viscous pinkish slime from its half-translucent form as it struggled upward to escape.

But Holmes merely strolled forward and casually tapped the curtain with his stick. Immediately the light fell. The scene had disappeared, and we were looking again at a plain gray curtain. Behind it Holmes's stick rapped solidly against the wall.

"Great Scott!" I began. "Is it..."

"It is the contents of *your* mind," said Crowley sharply. "Now you see there is danger in the saying, 'Seek and ye shall find.' "

"Your demonstrations are most diverting," said Holmes. "But you have not divined the main purpose of our visit."

"Have I not?" said Crowley, with exaggerated politeness. He lodged his formidable bulk in a thronelike chair with a high carved back and ornate arms. "Very well. Perhaps you are not the perfect guests, but I shall be the perfect host. Will you sit down, gentle-men?"

I sank with relief onto the sofa, as far from Crowley as possible, and Holmes took a chair in between.

"Will you have a glass of port, Dr. Watson?" Crowley went on. "The night has been a hard one for you, I see."

He indicated a graceful little glass of cut crystal filled with ruby-red wine, sitting upon the table just beyond my elbow. I reached gratefully to pick it up, only to have it dissolve beneath my fingers.

Crowley laughed. His huge open mouth seemed to take up half his face. Even Holmes raised an eyebrow in my direction.

"To return to serious business, gentlemen," Crowley said. "You challenged me to read the real intent of your thoughts, Mr. Holmes. Let me see..."—he closed his eyes and let his head loll against the collar of his cape—"I see leafy green trees, medieval towers, and guarded treasure. I see threats and fights, a group of men meeting in secret, a fat and pompous enemy..." He opened his eyes abruptly and stared at us with his eyes on parallel lines, giving the impression he looked right through us. "I see, you are thinking of Sherwood Forest, Mr. Holmes, with yourself in the role of Robin Hood. Though you are accompanied by an un-usually stupid Friar Tuck."

"See here, Crowley," I declared, recovering myself a little. "You make a very fine Sheriff of Nottingham yourself."

"Can't you do better?" added Holmes, coolly lighting his pipe. "Your humor is a cover for your ignorance, Crowley, though your reputation suggests more than a laughing buffoon."

"Of course I can do better," snarled Crowley. "You have been at Cambridge, investigating some matter. You have discovered that I know some of the persons involved, and you wish to query me about them. Do you think I am leading them astray? Am I the pied piper, making your scholars play truant? Perhaps the vice-master has enlisted you, Mr. Holmes, as one of his bulldogs."

"How could you lead them astray?" murmured Holmes, loung-ing back in his chair with a look of greatest indifference. "You are in disrepute at Cambridge. You left without taking your degree. You had no friends; you were not invited to join the Apostles. Who would receive you?"

"Base charges and ignominious lies," said Crowley. "I left without that useless piece of paper called a degree because Cambridge had done its work, molding my mind to the highest pitch of independent thought. I had no need for that crapulous credential. And as for the Apostles, they are but a silly society of simpering students and doddering dons. The greatest minds are outside its ranks, and it is among these that I make my friends."

He looked at us with disdain, but his hand closed upon a dangerous-looking device from the nearby table. It was a long steel spike suspended from a little network of straps. He fingered its needle-sharp point, and I realized with a start that Holmes lay stretched out languidly in his chair, in a pose of almost total vulnerability.

"Holmes!" I cried. "The dagger!"

"This?" roared Crowley, impaling it sharply in the floor. "What typical British ignorance. Have you never seen an up-to-date mountain climber's spike? With these upon my feet, I can ascend any glacier in the world with more rapidity than your pusillanimous Englishman can stroll up a grassy hill." And he roared with laughter, shaking his massive sides until his chair tottered.

Holmes waited coolly for him to subside, and then went on as if there had been no interruption. "I should rather say the Apostles are the height of eminence. What can be more distinguished than the mind of Keynes, say, or Russell?" And he stared blandly in Crowley's face.

"Keynes, the stock-market manipulator? He is interested in nothing but a game that he might turn to profit. His brains are trivial, though his character is not entirely without interest. It is said that at Bloomsbury he entertained the company by copulating in the drawing room with Vanessa Stephen, the sister of the lady novelist Virginia Woolf. I trust I do not embarrass you by mentioning this before your companion, Mr. Holmes." Crowley waved a deprecating hand at me.

"I assure you, Crowley," I declared roundly, "I am embarrassed only for the reputation of the lady in question. I should think it would embarrass anyone who would repeat such a slander."

"You *should* think," said Crowley. "I recommend you try it

sometime. No doubt it would embarrass you further if I were to speak of the practices that Keynes and Lytton Strachey have introduced into the Apostles."

"You cannot say the same of Russell," said Holmes. "Nor can you question his eminence, political, social, or intellectual."

"Russell is a prig," said Crowley, leaning forward in his chair. "Shall I tell you about the most modern and liberated affair he had with Lady Ottoline Morrell? It went on for some years, and during all this time he had trench mouth. With its stench I am sure you are acquainted, Dr. Watson. But he remained in ignorance of this fact to the end. Whether this speaks more for their physical ardor or for the deadly stoicism of the decadent aristocracy, I should leave to your conjecture."

"You go too far, Crowley!" I cried. "Such insults are not to be tolerated, I warn you."

"The Apostles are nothing," said Crowley, without so much as a glance in my direction. "It is not in their ranks that you will find the greatest minds, such as my friend Ludwig Wittgenstein. He is a Jew, with all the brilliance and all the nervous sensibilities of his race. He is, in fact, a bundle of twitching tendons and knotted nerves. He can write a treatise of the utmost profundity, but he cannot pour himself a cup of tea. Yet all the better, for it keeps him from the decadent company of his English inferiors. I hope to settle him somewhat by the widening experience and wholesome exercise of a tramp in foreign parts."

"I see," said Holmes. "And do you expect to embark soon together?"

"Our plans are not yet formed, Mr. Holmes, though I see no reason why I should tell you if it were otherwise. For Wittgenstein is the man you are trying to trace, is he not? You have been hired by Russell and Keynes and Moore and all that lot, to dissociate me from him, so he can do their work for them. Is that not so, Mr. Sherlock Holmes?"

"A very good guess, Crowley. Or is this not merely a good performance, expectable from one as devious as yourself, to throw off suspicion from your main purpose: to steal these young thinkers' ideas?"

"Ridiculous," said Crowley. "I have no interest in publication of that sort. I write poetry primarily, and my publications are in the main in that vein. You will hear them acclaimed when the world is elevated enough to appreciate them, for I am not only the greatest mountain climber in the world, but also the greatest poet. I have not lost my scientific habits of mind, but I apply them to matters higher than those that exercise most of my Cambridge brethren."

"Yet some of these works are extraordinarily interesting," Holmes persisted. He took a paper from a nearby pile. It read:

$$\int_0^a e^{-a^2}dx = \tfrac{1}{2}\pi^{\tfrac{1}{2}} - \frac{e^{-a^2}}{2a+} \frac{1}{a+} \frac{2}{2a+} \frac{3}{a+} \frac{4}{2a+} \ldots$$

$$4\int_0^\infty \frac{xe^{-x\sqrt{5}}}{\cosh x}\,dx = \frac{1}{1+} \frac{1^2}{1+} \frac{1^2}{1+} \frac{2^2}{1+} \frac{2^2}{1+} \frac{3^2}{1+} \frac{3^2}{1+} \ldots$$

"Surely this might attract some notice in scientific circles?"

"I did not claim to write it," said Crowley. "It is the work of a brilliant young Cambridge mathematician, Srinivasa Ramanujan. Knowing my own mathematical talents, he gave me some of his works to read on my recent visits to Trinity College."

"And do you expect to see him again?"

"When next I visit Cambridge, surely."

"That will not prove possible, I fear. Ramanujan is dead."

"Dead?" said Crowley, with a look of bland surprise. "That is tragic indeed. Yet it is not entirely unexpected. He had been in poor health, doubtless as the result of our barbarous British cuisine."

"Doubtless," said Holmes. "Yet death is such a mysterious process. It seems to have causes beyond our ken."

"It does indeed, Mr. Holmes. And whereof one cannot speak, thereof one must keep silent."

"You are evasive, Crowley. You are more involved with these Cambridge intellectuals than you admit. I happen to know that you have had dealings of a business nature with John Maynard Keynes."

"I have," said Crowley, "though the matter is rather above ordinary comprehension. But I will explain it to you. Keynes has

been attempting to purchase the complete occult writings of Sir
Isaac Newton, and who could be better equipped to find such
materials than myself?"

"Who indeed?" said Holmes. "The rest of us have passed ahead
into the twentieth century."

"It is I who have passed into the twentieth century," said
Crowley, drawing himself up to his full height on his throne.
"The rest of you are still in the nineteenth, with your narrow
sciences and your puerile atheism. I admire honesty, Mr.
Holmes, and I will be honest with you. I am the leading mind of
my generation. I have gone through all of its changes. Once I too
was an atheist, and combatted Christian bigotry and superstition
along with Bertrand Russell and Annie Besant. But their reform-
ism degenerated into such dreary diversions of outdated mor-
alism as educating the working poor and supporting the trades'
unions. I have outgrown their radicalism. It served for a time to
kill the Father, and bring that era to an end. It has not yet occurred
to them that a new era has dawned, and with it a new religion, that
of the Child."

"Indeed," said Holmes. "What is this new religion?"

"I would not speak of it further," said Crowley stiffly. "It is a far
more serious matter than any we are discussing."

"No matter. Your new religion, of course, is Theosophy. Annie
Besant has preceded you along that path."

"Surely you jest, Mr. Holmes. Even you must have heard of a
higher level of mystical organization than that."

"You mean the Order of the Golden Dawn."

"Exactly, Mr. Holmes. It introduces one to some aspects of the
ancient wisdom, at least above the level that the followers of
Madame Blavatsky and Mrs. Besant had been able to acquire. I
quickly learned what it had to offer, and rose to the top of its
ranks, the seventh degree. It is merely an intermediate level, but it
served, at least, to reveal to me my natural aptitude for magick."

"Did you not encounter any compatible company there?"

"The company was disappointing. It comprised such silly characters as the Irishman William Butler Yeats, with his vain preten-
sions to poetry. An inferior versifier he, compared to my majestic
themes and alliterated allegros. The leadership of the order was
pretended to by MacGregor Mather, and it was his incompetence

that brought the order to an end. For he himself held only the seventh degree, and he could not initiate the rest of us above that level. Eventually I received instructions from a higher source, and was told to take over leadership of the Golden Dawn from Mather. He was then living in Paris, where I delivered my instructions, and at first he agreed. Later he retracted, and we fought a magick duel, he in Paris, and I in Scotland."

"And where is Mather now?"

"He is dead."

"And you take credit for this?"

"My account is full," said Crowley. "I have no need of credit, Mr. Holmes."

"And so the Golden Dawn is no more?"

"It has been supplanted by a new order, the Argenteum Astrum, the Order of the Silver Star. I am its head, and I am empowered to initiate those who wish to advance to the highest levels of the magick arts."

He paused and stared right through us, his unconverging eyes glowing strangely.

"Perhaps you would like to try, Mr. Holmes? It involves a number of disciplines and ordeals, for nothing noble is gained without effort. But you have already made some progress just in reaching this room, passing through the labyrinth below. Will you not now go farther? I will show you the way. Not Watson, of course. You would be unsuitable. Your presence here means nothing. To fly through an ordeal on another's coattails is not valid. And it is exceedingly dangerous. You will undoubtedly fail to survive any further stages, should you be foolish enough to try."

Only Holmes's peremptory glance kept my lips sealed.

"It is not in my line," said Holmes. "I am a man of science. I have little interest in costumes, and foreign-sounding names, and concoctions from the blood of a toad and the wing of a bat. And still less in the sordid rites in which human *merde* is poured on the altar, or those in which a ghostly being is invoked at the sacrifice of a human child."

"Your acquaintance with magick is superficial, Mr. Holmes. Perhaps you have the acumen to recognize that I pronounce the word as I spell it, ending with a final letter 'k.' Those who dabble in black masses, like those fools in Paris a few years since,* and those benighted creatures of medieval times who indulged in human sacrifice in hopes of acquiring riches—they knew neither how to spell magick nor to practice it. They reverse the sacraments of the Catholic mass, thinking there is some significance in their blasphemous acts. They do not see that it is only to lend energy to their operations that they desecrate all human and holy values—the energy of their own emotions. But I use a more profound method. Violence is sordid, entrapping, unpleasant. I use a positive force—to be sure, one that also holds the danger of entrapping its user, but that does not happen if one remains master of it. It does take great strength of will, and even with this, one must be prepared for the spirits one invokes to appear sometimes in the guise of demons."

"These are words and figments of your mind," said Holmes, sitting back in his chair. "It is not science, for science deals only with facts."

"So it does," returned Crowley, "and so do I. But some facts are beyond the ken of narrow-minded scientists—not because the facts are uncommon, but because they are too intimate, too close to the self for them to notice. Take the moral beliefs on which you pride yourself—you especially, Dr. Watson, but you also, Mr. Holmes. Do they not resonate somewhere in your chest, and in your belly? And of what do they consist? Ideas and emotions. To be specific, fear of the human crowd whose fellowship you wish so desparately to keep, and anger against whoever seems to threaten its sway. That is what your morality is—the tones in your mind and body that tell you that you must be one of the pack, in order not to be one of its victims."

Holmes only stared at the ceiling, while Crowley went on.

"Or take the tone in here right now, gentlemen. Do you not feel a slight buzzing in the air? Is there not a rather high-frequency hum? No doubt you sense it, Holmes. Do you, Dr. Watson? If not, close your eyes and concentrate. We shall stop talking."

I did not wish to obey his orders. But Holmes was silent, and

---

* I.e., the followers of the Abbé Boullan, one of whom, Joris Karl Huysmans, described their activities in his novel *Là Bas* (Paris, 1891).—Ed.

the lateness of the hour made it easy in a few seconds to close my eyes. I listened to the silence, a silence largely filled, as it seemed, with the voice of Aleister Crowley.

"Do you not begin to notice now, Dr. Watson, an entire spectrum of sound? Do you hear a high-pitched, tiny, tinkling sound, like the fizz of electricity itself? We are told by our leading scientists that the world is made up entirely of electricity, as you know, of tiny positive and negative charges whirling about. Perhaps eventually they may advance far enough to know that their electric particles are themselves composites, compounds of still tinier entities flying rhythmically in and out of the void of nonbeing, and to know that all our world twists back upon itself in space and time, like wormholes in an apple."

Crowley's voice had a curiously soothing effect. He spoke more quietly now, slowly, in almost a purring tone.

"Now listen to the other end of the spectrum. Heavy sounds, deep and slow. The sound of traffic in the distance. The sound of your own blood. You can hear it easily if you draw yourself back inside."

A rhythmic pounding occupied my attention, very close to me. It was I. It was my heart, and my blood surging through the arteries. Somehow my attention had drawn itself up to my head, while my body sat there below like a zombie. I could feel the pumping of my heart, but the connections downward from my brain seemed to have frozen. I could not move a single muscle, nor would I have wanted to do so. Only my eyes were under control, for I could open and shut them, and look about the room.

Crowley's voice went on.

"There are higher vibrations than these, gentlemen. You are experiencing only the animal being, the body of nerve and gland played upon by the politician and the crowd-pleasing orator. Actors play upon it too, but in a higher sense, for they do so for the sake of artistry. And of course men and women—they play upon each others' susceptibilities, and thus cloak themselves in the most beautiful illusions that they can. And even above this we can rise. I belong to a profession of masters in this realm. Mere priests are at the bottom of our ranks, playing their games of moral feelings upon the nerve strings of membership in the human crowd. But we are of the highest: we are the magicians, the enlightened."

My consciousness had receded still farther. I looked down at the room from an angle above my eyes and far to the back of my head, as if I were sitting upon the mantelpiece. The room was quiet at last. Everything was in its place—there the tables with their heaps of books, there the heavy furniture, the gray silk rugs upon the wall, the little pillows of purple and scarlet brocade. There was Holmes, deerstalker cap upon his head, but without his usual pipe, sitting still as a rock. Across the room, Crowley sat in the midst of his robes, his face huge, fleshy, uncanny. Something tugged at the back of my head, where the autonomic nervous system controls one's heart and stomach and lungs and all the rest of the vital processes. I was not sleepy now, but wide awake, yet I could not move. My mind flashed across the possibility that something was happening to my body itself.

My thought was interrupted by a stronger tug.

The top of my skull seemed no longer solid, and I realized with a sudden thrill that I might recede through this hole. Crowley was trying to pull me right out of my body!

I resisted with all my might. But still I perched inside the back of my head, and still the tug continued. I could not move, nor open my lips to speak. How long could I hold on?

Then came a stranger sensation yet. It was a voice, Crowley's voice, though he sat across the room with lips that did not move.

Come now, Dr. Watson, it said. I have your mind under my control. Not that I should want it, except perhaps some day to chronicle *my* exploits. You do that sort of thing well enough.

Confound it, I thought to myself, how can this happen? How can this man get inside my head? And how can he drag my mind outside?

Quite simple, Dr. Watson, came the reply. We are on the astral plane, the locus of many phenomena. You are experiencing an instance of short-range telepathy, and you are concerned that you will leave your body in an astral projection. Do not be concerned. You will find it a most enjoyable experience.

I resisted with all my will. Yet Crowley's will was stronger. Gradually I felt myself slipping. The hole in my skull grew wider, and I started to be pulled through it into empty space.

Then came a second voice.

It was Holmes. One moment, Crowley, it said. You are not the only one who can play this telepathic game. You are wondering, Watson, how you happen to hear me as I am communicating with Crowley? I have made this a three-way circuit, for your convenience. Simply remember, Watson, astral projection is an act of will. He cannot pull you out, unless you want to go. He is merely showing you the way, and gulling you as to its inevitability. Hold on, old fellow. It is ultimately all in your mind.

It is indeed in your mind, said Crowley's voice. But do you suppose that your mind stands by itself? Do you not realize that your mind is not your own? You think in words that you have not invented yourself, words that are the property of others. Your thoughts are made up of things that you must say when you converse in the group, and your feelings are but eddies in the pool of group vibrations that wash continuously upon you. Your self-control is an illusion. You are part of this ocean around you. Do you not feel it, in the core of your being? Those high-pitched hums, those rumbling metal cars in the street outside, the pumping of your blood, do you hear them?"

I did. They pounded in my ears. The world was upon me, outside was inside, and I was about to leave my petty location in the corner of that room to join the rest of my greater being.

Hold on, Watson! I shall deal with him myself. It was Holmes. But he sounded more faint and distant, and his words faded away at the end. The pressure at the top of my head was immense, and I began to fly out. The room blurred, and murky shapes flashed by, and strange lights, and I shook to the vibrations of a thousand eerie sounds. A long cord stretched from me to my body, and it stretched ever longer and thinner, like a rubber band about to break.

Then the cord snapped back, and zounds! I was back in my body, sitting in an easy chair. There was the cheery fireplace, and the heavy brocade pillows, and Holmes, deerstalker cap and all, sitting placidly in his place.

"Holmes!" I cried. "You brought me back."

"I cut off his attention, Watson. But I have not learned what I wished to know. He is far too clever, and his will is too strong. The barrier is impenetrable."

Crowley's chair was empty. He was gone. We walked out of the room and into the great empty corridor.

Crowley's voice called out as we reached the top of the stairs.

"You wish to understand Cambridge? Seek the answers in London. Seek what is in that which is not. Seek the Scarlet Woman!"

But peer as we would, no further figures could be seen, material or immaterial. We trod back through that dismal labyrinth without further interruption. The front door opened noiselessly and of its own agency. Only as we crossed the threshold into the cold night air did we hear a voice ring out in a clanging malicious echo: "Goodnight, Mr. Sherlock Holmes."

CHAPTER 14

The Circle of the Damned

Our humble parlor at Baker Street was a welcome relief the next morning. So was the teapot, and the breakfast tray, and the sight of Mrs. Hudson herself, plain and dowdy in her smock. Only the set of Holmes's jaw gave a hint of the rigors of the night before.

"It was a night's work, was it not, Watson?" he said across the breakfast table.

"Is that what you call it?" said I, buttering my toast. "I should rather say it was a night at the chamber of horrors."

"I can see how it might appear so. Please forgive me, old fellow, for having made a guinea pig of you. I wished to draw him out, to make him reveal his methods. And I have a good idea now what they are."

"Telepathic suggestion, you mean."

"Yes, that, and the suggestible powers of drugs."

"Drugs, Holmes? I saw no such things in the house."

"But you inhaled them as we came up the stairs. Very cleverly done, I might add. He fogged our sense of smell in the lower rooms, while distracting us with his curiosities, and then gradually increased the dosage so as to make it almost imperceptible. The admixture of other smells was a nice touch. Those scents took me back a good many years, Watson. I had hoped never to encounter them again."

"But what drugs were they?"

"Opiated hashish, I should say, and also perhaps fumes derived from burning the crystals of cocaine. It is apparent that Crowley is a man of great wealth."

"So that is how he preyed upon Wittgenstein. He must have introduced him to a mystical cult, and thus built up his receptivity to various drugs under the guise of incense?"

"Very probably so, Watson. Later Wittgenstein might have taken to using drugs explicitly, hence the brown package in his safe. But I conjecture that Wittgenstein has attempted to tear himself away from the habit, or else Keynes's attempt to take over the drug ring removed this from Crowley's control, whereupon Crowley began to work upon Wittgenstein by telepathic suggestion."

"Indeed! This is a nefarious business, Holmes."

"Yes. We may have established Crowley's technique, then. But the puzzling part remains his motive."

"He could be using telepathic powers to engage in mental larceny, to steal the newest ideas of the intellectual elite."

"I thought so once, but now I have discarded that hypothesis. Crowley's answers last night show that he regards himself as proceeding in a more exalted direction. What did emerge was his dislike of Russell, and of British philosophers in general, perhaps also of the Apostles. I think it may be a case of revenge over some slight from long ago."

"Indeed, Holmes. Yet if so, why has he waited so long to avenge himself?"

"Perhaps he has only now acquired the means to act. But your objection has point, Watson. I am not convinced that revenge, or revenge alone, is all that is involved in this case. But one thing is clear. Crowley will not be crossed, and that is what worries me the most. How far will he go?"

"You mean how many targets will he strike?"

"Or how hard will he press when he encounters resistance. You recall the fate of the swarthy genius, Ramanujan."

"Ramanujan, of course! How forgetful one becomes on these intellectual heights. Was he killed by Crowley?"

"I am sure of it."

"But Crowley certainly did nothing to indicate it. He said that

Ramanujan was his friend, and that he hoped to see him again soon. He did not seem to know he was dead."

"That is exactly my point, Watson. Crowley was making a great deal out of reading our minds, if you recall. So I purposely thought of Ramanujan's death. Crowley must have noticed that, and yet he went out of his way to disguise the fact. That is a clear admission that he has something to hide on that score."

"But why should he kill Ramanujan?"

"Crowley must have wished to include him in his plot, but somehow they crossed purposes, and Crowley began to work against him telepathically."

"But surely Ramanujan was in his own element there. Could he not put up resistance?"

"Doubtless Ramanujan had psychic powers of his own, perhaps even greater than Crowley's. But he was not at the top of his form. He was weakened by this foreign climate and diet, and by the opiates with which Crowley and Keynes supplied him. It was another magick duel, and Crowley was again the victor."

"Then it is murder, Holmes! Ought we not to notify the police?"

"And tell them what, Watson? They will laugh us from court. No, we must continue our own investigations. I think we must look further into the question of accomplices."

"You mean Keynes, of course."

"To some extent, Watson. Granted, we have no strong proof that his brown package contained drugs, but it is a likely inference. And Crowley seemed rather to admire his alleged doings among the younger Apostles, and at Bloomsbury. Perhaps we should look further into the sexual element as well. It has just the tone of outrageous adventure that would appeal to Crowley. And around the Apostles there might have been a jealous masculine triangle that would provide the motive for Crowley's actions."

"I do not quite understand you, Holmes. And from your drift, I do not believe I entirely wish to."

"Then let it pass, Watson, let it pass. It may not prove relevant. If we can take Crowley, the rest will fall away like leaves when the tree is gone. Or perhaps only like smudges upon our spectacles."

"I should see it rather differently, Holmes. If you ask me, Whitehead is our man. He is the silent, self-centered genius of this operation, the Professor Moriarty of this latter age. His motive is jealousy of being surpassed by his former pupil, Russell, and by Russell's pupil, Wittgenstein; and Ramanujan was struck down because he was the friend and ally of Russell's political sympathizer, Hardy. Crowley, the pompous braggart, is only Whitehead's tool. There you see, Holmes, my hypothesis ties together all the facts and provides a plausible motive all around. Whitehead makes an excellent villain—vain, inscrutable, brilliant. And it is good clean criminality and does not require us to muck about in the obscene waters surrounding Aleister Crowley."

"Would it were so," said Holmes, turning to scan the papers. "Would it were so."

Next morning's mail brought a pair of letters from Cambridge. The first was from Russell. It read:

> DEAR HOLMES:
>
> I have managed to get a copy of the coroner's report, and I send it in an accompanying envelope. Keynes was kind enough to provide it. It is discouragingly uninformative, I fear. But I continue to hope that you will pursue the matter. You know my estimate of its importance. I can do very little, for I have taken on a rather heavy schedule of political work. The European crisis is worsening steadily, and we English are acting more and more like bulldogs, that is to say, bulldogs growling ever more furiously over a contested bone.
> Please carry on.
>
> My best wishes,
>
> RUSSELL

The second was a brief official document:

> Srinivasa Ramanujan, native of Madras, died at approximately 6 P.M. May 11, A.D. 1913, at Cambridge. Cause of death adjudged to congenital defects of constitution, together with the stress of an alien environment.
>
> J. DOOLITTLE, M.D.   Certified: D. DOGBERRY,
>   Constable

Below was written in black ink:

> On the basis of the above, the convening of an inquest
> has been judged not to be necessary.
> J. NEVILE KEYNES,
Justice of the Peace

"So!" I declared, throwing the paper upon the breakfast table. "Keynes has played his cards well. Nevile Keynes is his father,* is he not? Do you suppose the report has been falsified?"

"No," said Holmes. "It may be a report from a dubious hand, but I am inclined to believe it is correct, as far as it goes."

"But you still believe this was murder."

"I am more convinced than ever. And what a dangerous murderer he is, this man who strikes from afar! No, I think no one will be safe until we run him to earth."

"But how can we convict him of it, Holmes? The one man who can positively testify, other than Crowley himself, is dead. But of course if he were not dead, then he would have nothing to which to testify."

"A pretty dilemma, Watson," said Holmes with a smile. "You are becoming quite a Cambridge paradoxer yourself. But you do suggest to me a course of action. It would be difficult, but perhaps with your help it could be done."

"I am ready," I declared stoutly. "Tell me what I must do."

"You must practice the occult arts, Watson. Then after a long and arduous apprenticeship, you may develop the power to call Ramanujan's shade from beyond the grave.'

"Must I?" I cried. "Surely you jest, Holmes."

"Not at all, old man, not at all. But no, I foresee a snag. Contacting the spirit would not be enough. We should have to make him appear in court. And I fear he may not serve. For if he lived a good life, he would have been absorbed into nirvana, and if he lived a bad life, he would by now have been reincarnated as a

---

* John Nevile Keynes was not only the father of John Maynard, but the chief administrative officer of the University of Cambridge.—Ed.

snake. And either way, I fear the jury would find him a disreputable witness."

"Ah, stuff and rubbish!" I declared. "I heard quite enough of that on the Afghanistan border. Those devils shouted their magic cries to make them invulnerable, but they fell before good British bullets soon enough."

"And so may Crowley fall as well," said Holmes. "But we have no solid evidence against him, and it would be dangerous to let him strike again. I think we must penetrate his defenses from within." And he sank into a bemused study before the fire.

The following morning we had a caller. It was Keynes, immaculate in his dark suit, with top hat and rolled umbrella in hand.

"I see you have been at your brokers' again," said Holmes.

"I have indeed," said Keynes. "Shall I conjecture how you have arrived at this conclusion, Mr. Holmes? Have I left a bit of ticker tape sticking upon my trousers?"

"Rather more elementary," said Holmes. "The newspapers have reported volatile activity in the commodities markets these last few days, and it seemed more than probable you would have a hand in it."

"Clear enough," said Keynes. "May I ask whether you continue your interest in the recent events at Trinity College?"

"I have given them some thought," said Holmes.

"Perhaps I could offer my opinion, then. I think there is nothing, really, of any significance for a man of your interests. Intellectuals are a peculiar lot, and they have little aptitude for matters that are concrete rather than abstract and cerebral. Wittgenstein is a most unusual man, the very prototype of the mad genius. His whims and sudden disappearances are becoming proverbial. For him, extraordinary behavior is perfectly ordinary. Russell, I think, takes it much too seriously. I have the greatest respect for Russell, you understand. But he is rather a crusader, a Don Quixote on the field of modern moral causes. He cannot bear to see anyone suffer, and I think this makes him overreact to some of the normal pains of others' lives."

"Perhaps," said Holmes. "And what is your estimate of the sudden death of Ramanujan?"

"A tragedy," said Keynes. "A major loss to Trinity, and to the world. But there was nothing out of the ordinary in it. You have seen the coroner's report?"

"I have."

"But you do not believe it, is that it? I assure you, Mr. Holmes, that Dr. Doolittle is a reliable man. And if you like, I can arrange for him to be corroborated by independent medical opinion."

"I do not doubt it, said Holmes. "But perhaps I could ask you a question of my own."

"Certainly," said Keynes.

"Your Cambridge characters fascinate me, and some information may sometime prove useful in my work. Tell me, do you know of an old Trinity undergraduate, contemporary with Russell, a man named Aleister Crowley?"

"Crowley!" said Keynes with a smile. "Why, yes. He has acquired quite a reputation for himself. 'The wickedest man in England,' he is called in the tabloid press. He made quite a row in Trinity not long ago."

"Indeed," said Holmes. "Concerning what?"

"Many undergraduates now are throwing over the taboos of established Christianity, and some of them formed a little group called the Pan Society. They think in some way to recreate the fresh, wholesome religion of ancient Greece. The college authorities, some of whom date back to the days when a Fellowship was a clerical monopoly, looked askance at the club, and when the Pan Society invited Crowley to speak at their meetings, the authorities tried to exclude him from the college. He pointed out that he is a life member of Trinity, and could not be kept out of its precincts. The vice-master was incensed, and he retaliated by banning the Pan Society, and attempting to discipline its members for blasphemy. But they were all of them too rich and eminent in their social backgrounds to touch, except for a poor scholarship student named Norman Mudd, who was sent down."

"Very edifying," said Holmes. "And tell me, did the members of the Pan Society advocate practices between men like those of the ancient Greeks?"

"They have outgrown our barbaric western inhibitions upon the physical expression of love between man and man, if that is what you mean, Holmes."

"It is," said Holmes. "Perhaps you could tell me if these inhibitions also have been outgrown in the ranks of the Apostles?"

"The Apostles have no inhibitions at all," said Keynes, "save those imposed by the search for truth and human decency. But perhaps you had better ask Strachey about that."

And with a few more words of desultory conversation, Keynes took his leave. Holmes waited until he could be seen in the street below, and took his cap.

"Are you coming, Watson? I think the movements of Professor Keynes might well be worth following this morning."

We had little difficulty in following Keynes as he hailed a cab. Holmes hailed another, and pursued the first at a discreet distance. Keynes drove straight to the Treasury, where he entered without a glance about. The guard seemed to recognize him as a familiar figure.

Holmes drew on his pipe for a moment.

"We could wait here, Watson, but I suspect we might learn more now by other methods. I think it is time for us to visit the Theosophical Society."

"The Theosophical Society, Holmes? Have we not had enough of spirits for the present?"

"It is not spirits that I wish to see," said Holmes, "but to enlist the intuition of the very liberated Mrs. Annie Besant."

CHAPTER 15

An Astral Spy

The Theosophical Society occupied a large building on Avenue Road, in the quiet and genteel district just off Regent's Park. It was a neighborhood that just then was inhabited by many wealthy and noble foreigners, and it was no surprise to find the strange emblem of Theosophy on a street that contained so many crests and coats of arms upon its grand motor cars, and here and there upon an old-fashioned coach.

Going up the steps, we encountered a tall, stout gentleman with a thick walrus moustache just coming out the door. He seemed surprised to see Holmes, and merely tipped his hat with a slight shrug of his shoulders and then passed quickly into the street. Holmes, for his part, contented himself with a brief "Good morning, Dr. Doyle," and an ironic hint of a smile.

"Who is that gentleman?" I enquired. "I take it that you are acquainted."

"He is Arthur Conan Doyle," said Holmes, "a medical doctor with a small practice and much time on his hands. He occupies himself with various minor pursuits, among them an interest in psychic phenomena. I had forgotten that I might encounter him here."

"But is there some reason for you to avoid each other? I could not help but notice the strained tone of the encounter."

"We are relatives, after a fashion. But I have left his house long ago, and my career in the world is now my own business. There is no point in trying to pass backward over that gulf." And the set of his jaw told me that any further attempt at discussion on that topic would be futile.

In the anteroom, a fastidious young man in pince-nez eyeglasses sitting behind a desk asked us our business, and bade us wait until Mrs. Besant could see us. Holmes would not sit down, but paced about the front rooms. To the left was a large lecture room with a podium and many rows of chairs, and a bulletin on the wall announcing evening lectures on various aspects of Theosophy, principally by Mrs. Annie Besant, but also by the Reverend C. W. Leadbeater, and others.

In the room to the right, Holmes stopped before a chart upon the wall that gave the appearance of an anatomical diagram of some alien science. It showed the internal system of a man, but in place of the usual organs there were a series of colored circles, seven in all, connected by three winding tubes, and rising along the center of the body from the base of the spine to the top of the head.

"It is Oriental medicine, Watson," said Holmes, "the system of the chakras. They represent centers of energy, and hence of spiritual transformation, at different locations in the body. But this chart has a peculiarity that distinguishes it from others found in India and the East."

"Its peculiarity is that a civilized European should wish to display it in this country at all," I declared.

"My point was more medical than one of national bias," said Holmes. "You will observe that all the chakras are aligned in the center of the body, with one exception. They are placed at the crown, the forehead, the throat, the heart, the solar plexus, and the base of the spine, but one is set off to the left side of the abdomen."

"And the significance of this arrangement, Holmes?"

"It is the traditional Hindu system, but one chakra, that which centers on the genitalia, has been displaced to some more neutral organ."

"It has not been displaced," said a sharp voice behind us, "it has been placed correctly for the first time. There is no genital chakra, despite what certain corrupt texts declare. If there were, it would be exceedingly dangerous to arouse it. My own researches show that the correct designation is not the genital, but the *spleen* chakra."

Our speaker was an elderly man in a clerical collar, with a deeply tanned face and trembling hands. He took up his stance next to the chart, and seemed prepared to deliver us a considerable sermon.

"Doubtless you are Reverend Leadbeater," said Holmes. "I perceive you have spent many years in India, where you were subjected to tropical fever, and also to the esoteric doctrines of the Hindus."

Reverend Leadbeater started backward. "How can you know these things, sir? I am sure we have never met. You are, I presume, a clairvoyant."

"Rather simpler than that," said Holmes. "Your garb, your complexion, and your quavering hands proclaim these things, along with your circumstances here in this building. You were evidently once a missionary, but were yourself converted by the pagan wisdom of the East. And now you have returned to convert your homeland to your new faith—all except, of course, for the heresy of the genital chakra."

"Take care, sir, that you do not find yourself in its power!" declared the Reverend roundly. "It will mire you down to a miserable existence and a worse rebirth. Our meditations on the chakras should bring us upward, into the higher astral and mental planes."

"Doubtless you have much experience on these planes, Reverend?"

The clergyman drew himself up proudly. "I have written many books on them, sir, as has Mrs. Besant. Jointly we are proclaiming the entire esoteric truth to the world. Surely you know of my book *Man, Visible and Invisible*, or *The Other Side of Death*, or Mrs. Besant's work *The Self and Its Sheathes*?"*

---

* Reverend C. W. Leadbeater published some twenty books with the Theosophical Publishing House (Madras and London) between 1900 and 1930, including *Invisible Helpers* (1908) and *The Occult History of Java* (n.d.). Annie Besant published some thirteen books with them, ranging from *Ancient Wisdom* (1897) to *Man, Whence, How and Whither* (1913, in collaboration with Rev. Leadbeater).—Ed.

"All produced in automatic writing, and dictated by the Secret Chiefs in the Himalayas?"

"We have not produced Theosophical books in that fashion since the time of Madame Blavatsky," said Reverend Leadbeater in an offended voice. "We have carried on by our own strength. I should remind you, Madame Blavatsky has been dead some twenty years."

"What," said Holmes, "and not reappeared even once since then?"

"You mistake our mission, sir," said the Reverend, "which is to spread universal spiritual truth, and thus lead to the elevation of all mankind. Doubless séances have their place, but they belong to a more private phase, and for certain gifted individuals. Madame Blavatsky was strong in all phases of the work. She could produce materializations, messages from beyond, raps on the walls—she could dim a candle by merely pointing her finger. Once in Bombay, I witnessed her bring down a shower of rose petals out of the air upon a group of visiting dignitaries."

"It has been alleged," said Holmes, "that these things have been produced quite materially, by the use of secret panels in the walls. Did not Madame Blavatsky's own servants confess to this once?"

"She was unjustly accused by the jealousy of those who could not stand their own inferiority. Strong natures arouse strong undercurrents. The larger the wave, the larger the following trough."

"And this is the reason," said Holmes, "that you do not practice spiritualism, but only preach it?"

"I will rise to your challenge, sir," declared Reverend Leadbeater. He closed his eyes and began to sway from side to side, his facial muscles clenched intently. Presently we heard some sharp rapping in the walls, first to the left, and then to the right side of the room.

"Aha!" said Reverend Leadbeater, opening his eyes. "Did you hear that? I am quite sure you did."

"We heard some raps," said Holmes. "Were they yours?"

"Mine?" said the Reverend, blushing. "Well, I have hardly ever—it is all the doings of the spirit world, you know."

"Oh," said Holmes, "I thought perhaps it might have been Mrs. Besant thinking a bit too vigorously in the adjoining room."

"You shall see," murmured Reverend Leadbeater. And he closed his eyes again, and began to sway so heavily that I thought he might fall over. Then the inner door opened, and Annie Besant appeared.

"Did you rap, Reverend L.?" she called. "I have not heard you raise a rap in many years, and I felt it called out to me."

"It was the spirits, Mrs. B.," said Reverend Leadbeater. "I am privileged to be merely their medium. And as for calling out to you, perhaps these gentlemen..."

"Oh, Mr. Holmes," cried Annie Besant, "and Dr. Watson. How good of you to come. I *felt* you would come, you know, I *felt* I was needed. Is it about dear Mr. Russell? I felt he needed me a few days ago, but now his need of me seems transferred to you. Yes, I *feel* that most distinctly. Will you come in?" Her face flushed almost to match her red hair, with the anticipated pleasure of helping us, and she led us into her office.

The office of the director of the Theosophical Society was spacious, but crowded with strange artifacts. Annie Besant seated us in chairs near her paper-strewn desk, Holmes in a little alcove formed by a huge Egyptian urn and a tall Chinese screen, myself at a greater distance, between the urn and a large statue of a cat-faced goddess sitting very erect with hands on her knees. Around the room were other tables covered with papers, scrolls half-unrolled to reveal Egyptian hieroglyphics, another copy of Reverend Leadbeater's chart of the chakras, and, in one corner, a gramophone with a windup crank and a large brass horn.

"We are so busy with the external work of the society," said Annie, "so much correspondence from new lodges in Europe, sister lodges in America, and mother lodges in India. There are so many lectures, and yet we must find time for our spiritual inspiration as well."

"I have not forgotten your powers so soon," said Holmes. "I had hoped you might find time to aid us again."

"With all my heart," she cried. "What is the target of your searches now, Mr. Holmes?"

"I wish you would tell us what you know of Aleister Crowley and his occult organization, the Order of the Silver Star."

"Mr. Crowley is a very distasteful subject. He deals only with the lower chakras. Reverend Leadbeater will tell you of their

dangers. As for his organization, all I can say is that the Order of
the Golden Dawn broke off from the Theosophical Society some
fifteen years ago, when some of the members became more interested in the phenomena of séances than in the higher spiritual
and mental teachings. And subsequent history has borne us out,
Mr. Holmes. The Golden Dawn has been wracked by dissension,
and by the breaking off of other groups, such as Crowley's order,
which you referred to, whereas the Theosophical Society has
continued its work and gone on from height to height."

"Doubtless so," said Holmes. "Yet my task is to probe the
darkness, in order to combat it. Can you tell us no more about the
goals and practices of the Order of the Silver Star?"

"I do not know, Mr. Holmes, and I do not wish to know.
Crowley has only a degraded version of love, dealing with the
energies of the lowest physical plane. We deal with cosmic love,
the spirit that draws us out of ourselves and into the greater
Oneness of the higher planes. For Spirit itself is love. Do you not
agree, Mr. Holmes?"

"I could not say," said Holmes. "I have no factual evidence of
that phenomenon."

"Oh, but you will," smiled Mrs. Besant. "I feel sure of it."

"For the present," said Holmes, "I should be very glad of some
evidence regarding Crowley and his circle. Could you not turn
your inner vision to tracing his recent doings? It is a matter of great
importance, for many of our friends."

"It is dangerous to think too steadily on evil objects. One can
start channels flowing that may be reversed. We must guard
ourselves from such negativity."

And just then the urn between Holmes and myself trembled
from a loud rap within, as if to punctuate Mrs. Besant's emphatic
opinion.

"Very well," said Holmes. "Perhaps you could help in a more
limited way. I have just come from a visit with a gentleman who
seems involved in this case. Can you pick up his trace, and tell me
what you see of his doings?"

"Certainly," she replied, pulling her chair close to Holmes.
"Think of him now, and look steadily into my eyes."

"But Watson must remain here too," said Holmes, and would

not allow her to begin until she agreed that I might stay in the room, although I was under no circumstances to break my silence.

"I see him," said Annie presently. "Dark eyebrows, a wide and bristling moustache, dark suit, gold chain—there is much gold about him."

"That is the man," said Holmes. "What do you see of him?"

"He is concerned with something that he considers very valuable, something very material, some commodity to be consumed on the level of gross sensory pleasures. He is engaged in dealings and calculations, but it is something that he wishes to keep secret."

"Excellent, my dear Mrs. Besant. Who are his partners in these dealings?"

"It is unpleasant to look in that direction," she said at last. "I do this only for you, Mr. Holmes."

"Tell me, then, whom he deals with—no matter what you see."

"It is dark, evil, a wet and slippery underground. I can see no faces at all now, only some demonic energy. There are signs of struggle going on."

"Are they enemies, then?"

"Thieves have no honor even among themselves," sighed Mrs. Besant. "It is an uneasy relation, but now it is emerging into the light. I can see a face."

"A face? Whose?"

"*Yours*, Mr. Holmes." And with this, Annie Besant shook herself as if to refresh her energies, and blinked her eyes. An uneasy atmosphere pervaded the room. I noticed that the pictures and scrolls about the walls did not hang straight, although they had looked normal enough when we entered a few minutes before. The walls creaked uneasily, and a book fell from a table with a dull thud. The screen that partly shielded Holmes from my view was visibly shaking.

"I will go farther for your sake," said Mrs. Besant in a strange voice, "though it is fearful to do so."

"I appreciate your courage," said Holmes, "and I am grateful. What shall we do?"

"We must complete the circuit. You must stare into my left eye with both your eyes, and I shall stare into your right eye with both of mine. That will intensify the flow. Banish all thoughts, and soon you will see my face change. Remember well the image that appears there."

They leaned close together, intent upon this mutually hypnotic gaze. They seemed far away, behind a barrier of opaque air, though I sat but a few feet from them. The urn echoed sharply to a staccato rapping within, but still Holmes and his red-haired clairvoyant stared cooly into each other's eye. I glanced at the cat-goddess uneasily, for this statue towered above my seat, and it too seemed to be swaying uncertainly. Then the urn boomed like a blow upon a bass drum, and the Chinese screen fell down sideways, blocking Holmes and Annie Besant into a narrow alcove and sealing them entirely from view.

Annie's voice went on in a deeper, inner rhythm. "The forces are very strong now, dear Mr. Holmes. Come, let us both enter into it, and we shall see together all that might be wished!"

Her voice was throaty, loudly purring. I glanced at the cat-goddess beside me, and would not have been surprised at that moment to hear an answering purr. But all was silent in that quarter, and my attention was drawn back to a noise behind the screen that I could not have expected, even in that strange place. It was the sound of clothing rustling and even tearing, the sound of someone becoming disrobed. Mrs. Besant, already obviously in a deep trance, was acting more than her usual self.

Then came Holmes's voice, purring smoothly too, but with a strong and purposeful edge. "Very well," he said, "I have come this far with you, Annie, now you must come farther with me. You have seen the face of the man with the bristling moustache, the man who deals in a secret commodity. Who is his partner?"

Mrs. Besant moaned uneasily, as if disturbed in the midst of a dream.

"Look into the dark spot in Keynes's eyes," said Holmes. "What does he see? Is it Crowley?"

With that, Mrs. Besant screamed. The Egyptian urn gave a last, climactic rap and shattered into pieces. The screen fell from where it was propped between Holmes's chair and the desk, to flatten itself upon the floor and reveal the figures of Holmes and Annie Besant. He sprawled indolently in his chair, and she was stretched upon him with her clothes in a most compromising position. I turned my head.

Presently Mrs. Besant was back on her feet, and abruptly returned from her mystical rapture to the immediate scene. "Crowley," she repeated angrily, "Crowley. Why, he is here! The channel was open too long. Those were his raps, not mine!"

And she looked wildly about the room.

Holmes regained his feet with the utmost coolness, and strolled casually across the room to the gramophone upon its stand.

"If you will be silent," he said, "we could hear a sound coming from this." And he turned the horn toward us.

There was a faint sound coming from it, though the needle did not touch the grooves, nor did the record turn or the crank move. Then the sound grew louder and louder, and soon it filled our ears. It was the bellowing sardonic laugh we had heard that night at Chancery Lane. It was the laugh of Aleister Crowley, as he mocked us maliciously, victoriously, over the shambles of the room.

CHAPTER 16

Clouds and Shadows

No sooner had we left the Theosophical Society than we encountered a familiar figure in the street. It was John Maynard Keynes, with his top hat and umbrella, and he was walking briskly up Avenue Road. He had not seen us. Holmes placed a warning finger to his lips and beckoned me to follow.

At the corner Keynes hailed a horse cab, and stepped inside without a backward glance. As they started off, Holmes hailed another cab from the press of traffic. Its driver, a grizzled and misshapen old man, gave Holmes a look of something like recognition.

"Can you follow that cab wherever it goes?" cried Holmes. "There is half a crown if you never let it out of sight."

The driver grunted, and so we clambered aboard and were off.

"What a coincidence, Holmes!" I declared. "The very man we wished to inquire about, and now we find him here."

"Quite so, Watson. And if only you were in the habit of following your own train of thought to its proper conclusions, you would deduce something significant from that fact."

"Should I? What conclusion is that?"

"Elementary, Watson. Here is Keynes, not in his usual neighborhood of the Treasury or the City bankers, or even of his intellectual friends at Bloomsbury, but in this very leisurely and retiring quarter with its abundance of titled foreigners. What is he doing here? I leave it to your imagination."

"I do not see your drift. If we are to credit Mrs. Besant's clairvoyance, he should be engaged in some commercial transaction, and as you say, that would be more likely in some other neighborhood. Unless he is purveying exotic drugs to these elegant householders—is that what you mean?"

"Either that, or else his purposes here are more closely linked to ourselves than we know," said Holmes, clamping his teeth upon his pipe.

Keynes's cab proceeded at a leisurely pace along the great green meadows of Regent's Park. Presently we came out into the denser flow of horse cabs and trolleys of Marylebone Road, and the eddies made where these gave way to occasional motor cars. At Great Portland Street, Keynes's cab suddenly veered to the side and plunged into a bewildering series of maneuvers. It turned first left and then right, reversing direction and even recrossing its path, once circling entirely around the block. Clearly Keynes seemed to be trying to evade pursuit. But Holmes's driver, for all his sodden looks, was equal to the challenge. He wheeled his cab expertly through that maze, never letting his quarry quite disappear from sight.

Eventually Keynes must have decided he could not shake us off, for his cab set a straight course again, and without further tricks, proceeded along Euston Road. We were entering Bloomsbury, that neighborhood behind the University of London and the British Museum, shunned by the most respectable families but beloved of London's intellectuals and bohemians. The cab pulled up at a large house on Brunswick Square, and Keynes got down and went quickly inside. He seemed to be carrying something under his arm.

Our cab pulled up at a discreet distance as we watched the other cab drive off. "Excellent," said Holmes, as we alighted. "Doubtless you have recognized the neighborhood, Watson. You should not be surprised to know that this is the house where Keynes's old Cambridge friend Lytton Strachey lives in a communal arrangement with Virginia Woolf and her husband Leonard, her sister Vanessa, and a host of other relatives and friends. It is, in short, the home of that group of avant-garde intellectuals known as the Bloomsbury circle."

"Then perhaps Keynes has come to make a delivery to another

part of his drug ring," I said. "For I saw another of those packages under his arm."

"I saw no such thing," said Holmes with uncustomary sharpness. "And it hardly seems possible that you should notice a fact that I should overlook."

"I own you may be right, Holmes," I replied, "although you might credit me with an occasional observation. Certainly it is not my fault if you did not look closely for once."

Holmes clapped his hand on my shoulder. "Forgive me, old fellow. I should not have spoken to you that way. And I will admit there is something about this scene that makes me uneasy. But come, let us have a look at this house." And he led the way through an iron gate into a narrow alley that ran along the side of the building.

Some ways back, above a narrow flower bed, was a high window, closed and draped. From behind it came a series of strange noises. There were peeping and mewing sounds, like little animals snuffling about, and then the giggle of human voices.

"Give me a leg up," whispered Holmes. I hoisted him up to where he could reach the window sill, and he pulled his head over the ledge. Yet apparently the blinds were drawn too tightly, for in a few seconds he dropped back down, leaving a second pair of footprints beside my own in the damp soil.

"It is no good," he whispered as we retreated farther down the alley. "Nothing further can be seen from out here. We must find an entrance. I daresay we will scarcely be noticed."

"You see?" I cried softly. "There is no doubt of it. Keynes was making a delivery, and they are already in the early stages of intoxication. Their sounds betray it."

"Or else, Watson," he replied, softly slipping the latch on a screen door to a rear porch, "we have caught Keynes and his friend in one of those unnatural acts for which they made the Apostles famous. You may have heard of Lytton Strachey's nickname, 'the buggerer of Bloomsbury'?"

I could not reply to Holmes's distasteful remark, for he held a finger sharply against his lips and crept stealthily inside. And having even less desire to be found standing alone on the back steps of this infamous house than to accompany Holmes inside it, I had no choice but to follow.

We made our way down a dim corridor. A series of doors stretched off on both sides, and, farther down, another corridor intersected it at right angles. With unerring instinct, Holmes located a door and bent his eye to the keyhole.

I could not help reflecting on the sordidness of this case as we stood there, listening to the noises from inside the room. The giggles continued, and, with them an assortment of coos and bleatings and mewings, as if we were eavesdropping on a room full of beasts. What vile effects there were in that terrible intoxicant—or worse yet, Holmes might be right about the alternative. In either case, we were reduced to gathering evidence on a most disreputable network of practices, and by the almost equivalently disreputable method of peeping through a keyhole in the dark.

Then a light came on in the adjoining corridor, and footsteps came briskly toward us. We were about to be discovered.

Holmes straightened up, and without a moment's hesitation, decided upon his path of action. He opened the door and we both stepped inside.

There, in a cheerful, brightly hung room was a strange and unexpected sight. Keynes was nowhere to be seen. Instead, a man and a woman were lounging upon a rug before the hearth, making faces at each other and emitting little bursts of animal noises, interspersed with peals of laughter. In their childish play, they did not even hear us at first as we entered and shut the door. Then the woman looked up, and quickly climbed to her feet. She was very pale and very thin, with a face of exceedingly refined intelligence and exceedingly great beauty. Evidently this was the lady novelist Virginia Woolf. Her face flushed with anger, and she seemed about to break into a fit.

Her companion, however, did not seem perturbed at all, as he lounged against an ottoman. He wore curious rimless spectacles and had a long, pointed beard. His clothes were outlandish and ill-fitting upon his narrow frame. At first sight I would not have taken him for a gentleman.

"I am Sherlock Holmes, the detective," said my companion. "Doubtless you are Lytton Strachey, and this is the talented Mrs. Woolf. I should like to make some inquiries about your acquaintances."

Strachey gave a curious, high-pitched laugh. "Inquiries of criminal suspicion?" he said. "How delicious. Perhaps this will be a
strange new form of pleasure, sordidly to betray one's friends
under the guise of a search for truth."

"I do not deal in betrayals," said Holmes, "but only in facts."

"You are obviously a detective of the '90s," said Virginia Woolf,
taking a deep breath. "You combine Victorian arrogance with
Edwardian perversity. Surely your facts could be subordinated to
the courtesy of knocking upon the door—the one at the front of
the house where the servant can separate true visitors from common curiosity seekers."

"Forgive us, Mrs. Woolf," said Holmes. "We are very pressed,
and upon an important and rather mysterious matter. We came
here after your friend, Mr. John Maynard Keynes."

"I might have known as much," said Virginia Woolf.
"Maynard's charm, I fear, is the barrier gate between us and the
more dubious part of the world, and every now and again some of
it comes through the gate."

She turned abruptly on her heel and left the room, taking the
same door we had used, for there was no other exit.

"So," said Holmes, "Keynes seems to have escaped."

"Escaped?" said Strachey. "He was never here, not this morning, certainly."

Holmes moved to the window and glanced through the blinds.
From his expression I knew Strachey was right. The mud below
must show nothing more than our own sets of footprints, made as
we peeped from below. But Holmes's questioning wavered not a
moment.

"What a pity," he said. "Not to get today's delivery of hasheesh,
or perhaps a nice bit of heroin."

"Heroin?" said Strachey. "I have not heard about that before.
But hasheesh—you say Keynes has found some of that? It is the
herb glorious, the discovery that London owes to Paris, and Paris
to the Arabian nights. You think Keynes might bring some?" He
sat up with interest.

"Perhaps," said Holmes. "That is why I thought you might
know where Keynes is in this house."

"You believe Keynes is in the house?" said Strachey. "Curious,
he always steps in to see me first. And I am near the front door. I

can always hear it open. Yet no one has come in or out, this entire morning. What did *you* do, Mr. Holmes, climb in through some unguarded window?"

"It is hardly relevant. Perhaps I am mistaken. Yet I hope you would be willing to tell me something, if not about Keynes himself, at least about his connections. Do you know who sells him the drugs he brings?"

"I have no idea where Maynard picks up his exotic morsels, of any kind," said Strachey. "He is a man of wide and varied acquaintance, not many of whom I am likely to know."

"But some of them you might," said Holmes. "Tell me, do you not know Aleister Crowley?"

"I am not so decadent," said Strachey in a squeaky voice, "as to desire *his* company."

"Why not? I thought you rather admired the breaking of inhibitions upon primitive instincts, and even that the two of you might share some of the same tastes."

"Ah, Mr. Holmes. I fear there is a weak point in every philosophy, and Crowley is the weak point in mine. His is the pathology of the opposite extreme. He is restrained by nothing save the workings of his enormous ego."

"Was he never connected with the society at Cambridge known as the Apostles?"

"The Apostles? Certainly not. Crowley has always been a pompous ass. He would never be received in any intelligent circle."

"Let me be frank, Strachey. Do you suppose there has been any sexual entanglement between Crowley and any member of the Apostles?"

"To be frank, Holmes, no." Strachey shook his head with disgust. "If anyone would have knowledge of such a thing, it would be I. In a word, he is not our type."

"I believe you," said Holmes. "Then let me ask you another thing. I take it that Bertrand Russell has never engaged in any sexual practices in the Apostles?"

"No, Russell has the stiffness of his virtues. He would never indulge himself in any way."

"That is just my point. Russell is greatly admired, is he not? Is it possible that someone in the Apostles has fallen in love with him, in more than an intellectual sense, and has been disgruntled because he was rebuffed?"

"What a delightful idea," said Strachey. "I am coming to think you have possibilities, Holmes. But no, I can tell you truthfully that it is out of the question."

"Very well," said Holmes. "But Keynes and Crowley seem to find each other tolerably amusing, do they not?"

"Keynes is an adventurer. What he may do I cannot answer for. If he knows Crowley, he has his reasons, though I dare say they are not emotional or erotic ones. Keynes operates in realms that none of us ever enter. He is our link to the outer world, or I should say, the lower."

Lytton Strachey pulled himself to his feet and ushered us toward the door. "Bloomsbury is a little fairyland in the midst of this mundane world, you see. We are like children left on their own on equal terms with adults. This house belongs to the remaining sons and daughters of the literary editor Sir Leslie Stephen. They were left by the death of both parents at just the time they came into their majority, and so they have continued living together as a large, communal family, minus adults. They have taken some more of us into their ranks, college friends of the boys, such as myself, from Cambridge, and Leonard Woolf, who married Virginia. And Keynes, of course. Whatever Keynes may do elsewhere, when he is with us he is one of us. We are a group of literary talents, and free spirits, and nervous ticks, and all that it takes to make a paradise on earth. We may not change the world—none of us except Keynes, perhaps—but it shall not change us."

Strachey opened his door and saw us out. "Come and visit us, Holmes. You will see what we are about. At least, come and visit me."

Holmes seemed to have some inclination to search the house further, but I steadfastly held out for the front door, and presently we were outside again. The moist London air of that cloudy day seemed fresh by comparison with the atmosphere in the house. Here and there, little patches of sunlight even broke through the dreary sky.

Holmes's face, though, was shrouded with doubts. He looked

slightly ill, and I began, for once, to have worries about him in my own mind.

"Are you quite well, Holmes?" I began. "Come now, we have had a check, we have lost our track. What does it matter? We shall track Keynes again tomorrow, or this evening, whenever we find his trace."

"Doubtless so, my old friend," said Holmes. "I thank you for your kindness. I know how distasteful this line of inquiry is to you. But I think we must wait here, and pick up the track now, for Keynes is up to something, and the link leads right to Crowley. Have you so soon forgotten the events in Mrs. Besant's office?"

"I have not forgotten. But must we wait here for Keynes to come out? He may already have left."

"I do not think so, Watson. I do not feel it. But look!" And he pointed across the square. There was Keynes again, with top hat and umbrella, but minus any brown package, just stepping into another cab.

We quickly found a cab of our own. Holmes repeated his instruction to the driver, and once again we followed Keynes through the streets of London. But this time he made no effort to lose us, but drove steadily toward the river. Soon we had crossed Blackfriars Bridge and entered a neighborhood of docks and warehouses and dirty cafés. The two cabs easily kept within hailing distance. Suddenly Keynes stopped, and dismissed his cab in front of a dismal boarding house.

We stopped across the street and waited for him to come out. This he soon did, in the company of a second man, who was rather tall and morose-looking, with a dark, ugly face, and wearing a black suit. They turned the corner and began walking up the street. I saw that both of them held brown packages, rather like the one we had fought over at Trinity gate, but somewhat bigger. From the look in Holmes's eye, I knew that this time we were both seeing the same thing.

"No time for gloating, Watson, but only for action," he declared as we strode briskly after the two men. "No doubt you have recognized the second man. He fits the description Mrs. Besant gave us at Cambridge when she interrogated the messenger boy. He is Keynes's former partner."

"But how can these be working together, when they are on opposing sides of a conflict?"

"That is easily explained," said Holmes. "Business partners may fall out from time to time, and when that happens either they have recourse to lawyers and law courts or, if the business is an illegal one, they provide their own means of coercion. It comes rather to the same thing, you know. And reconciliations are sometimes enforced rather abruptly, by one method or another."

We picked our way through muddy streets, avoiding an occasional delivery wagon. Rain had fallen in little showers here and there in London, for the weather was nowhere the same that day, and the clouds blew raggedly across a windy sky. Here and there patches of sunlight fell upon the street and glinted from the puddles. Where it struck the peeling paint of the dilapidated warehouses, the light made them look even more dismal. Half a block ahead of us, Keynes and his companion skittered quickly through the sunlight and back into the shadows.

"I say, Holmes," I declared, "this is a back way into Waterloo Station. They must mean to take the train."

"Indeed they do," said Holmes. "And it is to be the boat train this time. I dare say they might lead us all the way to the Continent. And that is something I am very anxious to avoid!"

With these words, he broke into a run. At the next corner, he motioned to an alley running parallel to the street along which Keynes and his companion strode. Just a few blocks ahead was the station.

"Hurry, Watson," Holmes declared. "We may beat them to the next corner and turn them aside. Run!"

Run we did, Holmes effortlessly and in his strange leaping stride, I blustering along behind with heaving lungs. At the end of the alley, though, we found we had won the race, for we had reached the corner ahead of our opponents, and we stepped out to confront them almost face to face.

Keynes and the dark man did not seem eager to meet us. Without a word, they bolted sideways across the street, and ran up the block perpendicular to their original line of march. Holmes and I rushed after them, splashing through a few puddles in our haste, while the wind blew stronger and colder, and the clouds above seemed to career crazily across the sky.

Halfway down the block, the street was traversed by a narrow alley, and the pair split up, Keynes running to the left, the dark man to the right.

"Quick, Watson," Holmes cried, gesturing to the right. "Stop him, however you can. Use your revolver if you must!" And he dashed across the street and into the alley behind Keynes.

I turned to the right and saw my figure in the distance ahead. He was running clumsily, evidently in no better condition than I, and still he clutched the brown package under his arm. He looked back at me for the first time, and his face shone with some dark malignancy that made me cry out in disgust.

"Stop, man!" I cried. "Stop or I will shoot!"

But he did not stop, nor could I gain on him. He looked back again over his shoulder, and I clutched my revolver as a last gasp of sanity in this mad, endless chase. The dark man's face broke into a hideous smile, and I pulled the trigger.

The shot was true, for the body fell abruptly to the ground. I could not bring myself to approach it at more than an aching walk. Then he began to crawl, pulling himself to the corner of the wall, and collapsed out of my sight. The brown package was still in his hand.

I made as much haste to the corner as I could. There was nothing beyond but a little cul-de-sac at the back of two warehouses—and on the ground, nothing but mud. There was no body, no blood, no brown package. Worst of all, the sunlight flickering on the mud showed no marks. Nothing had touched the earth there at all.

I stared at my revolver. The shot at least was real: the barrel was warm, one cylinder was empty. My fatigue dissolved into a wave of panic, and I noticed not even any heaving of my lungs as I raced back down the alley and across the street where Holmes had gone in pursuit of his prey.

The path was simple on the other side. It ran straight ahead, and then hooked abruptly to the left. From the turn, I saw Holmes and Keynes outlined against a bare brick wall that ended the passageway. Keynes had turned to face his pursuer, brown package still in his hand. Holmes edged steadily closer to him, moving slowly and deliberately.

The wind howled tonelessly, and I felt a bit of rain in the air.

Then I saw that a patch of sunlight was sliding down the brick wall and that Holmes, with his inexorable advance, was maneuvering Keynes steadily into the sunlight. Then the sunlight struck them both, sending a pool of shadow from Holmes's feet across the bricks, but from Keynes's feet there was no shadow at all.

With a smile, Holmes reached out to take the package from Keynes. He shrank back before the detective's hands. *It* shrank back, for it was nothing but an apparition that faded into the bricks, and Holmes waved his empty hands for me to see.

"Great Scott, Holmes!" I cried. We have been led all this way by these figments of our minds?"

"Yes, Watson, but not figments of our minds alone. There is another mind from which they emanated, I am sure."

"Crowley's?"

"Yes, Crowley. If the sun had not come out today, we might have found ourselves chasing these apparitions across the Channel, to God knows where."

We picked our way back to more civilized parts and hailed another cab. "For good measure, let us check one more possibility," said Holmes. We crossed back over the Thames, and presently we pulled up before the Treasury. Holmes got down and spoke to the policeman on duty.

"Professor Keynes?" said the officer of the law. "He has been within since ten o'clock this morning, sir. I'm afraid I cannot admit you without special authorization. It's quite an important financial consultation going on. No, sir, he has not left even once, though they did send out for lunch. Why, thank you, sir"—and we left him with a bemused smile on his face, and a shiny half crown in the palm of his hand.

"It has led to nothing," said Holmes as we returned home. "We shall have to approach Crowley's operations in another way, and this may not prove easy. I believe I know what Crowley has done, but I have no proof. We must catch him in the midst of his operations, and that may take time." And he lit his pipe and settled back with a look that showed he was prepared to wait for a very long time indeed.

CHAPTER 17

The Mark of the Beast

We waited, Holmes scanning the psychic horizons now as well as the usual annals of crime. The spring sun went away, and the fog came in, and the rain, and then the cold, and the snow, and the wet leaves and again the rain and fog. Russell's premonitions were true; war came nearer and nearer on the Continent. Still Holmes silently scanned the horizon.

One morning, reading through the *Times*, I made my own contribution to the case.

"Look at this, Holmes," I remarked, and passed the paper across the breakfast table. I pointed to a curious notice in the advertisement column.

> Musician, female, needed for high ceremony.
> Experience essential. Deus diabolis 666 = 711. Large
> reward. Contact the *Times* number 323.

"It appears to be a message from Crowley, is it not? He must be planning another magick ceremony. If we can reach his assistant, we will be able to investigate his operations from within. If only there is some way to discover who answers the advertisement. We must contact the *Times*."

"We shall indeed," said Holmes. "But there is no need to inveigle the publishers into revealing who answers this advertisement."

"Why not, Holmes? It is our only chance."

"Because I placed it there myself."

Holmes returned late that afternoon and reported he had arranged a meeting. At seven o'clock the following evening, we were sitting in a supper club in Soho, a rakish style of establishment such as seemed to have sprung up in the last few years, where intoxicants stronger than alcohol were rumored to be available.

Holmes poked at his chop in silence, and my efforts to draw him into conversation came to nothing. At last, twenty-five minutes after the hour, a woman appeared.

"You're Mr. Holmes, aren't you? I came in answer to your telegram. I'm Leila Waddell."

She was a slender girl in her mid-twenties, with large brown eyes and brown hair worn straight, parted in the middle and falling almost to her hips. It covered her shoulders front and back, but it did not disguise the low cleft of her dress, or the strange mark that was drawn in red ink between her breasts, the mark we had seen on the emblem in Ramanujan's room:

"What instrument do you play?" said Holmes.

"The violin. How much do you pay?"

"It varies. How much can you do? How well can you fit in?"

"I can fit in, if I know what you want."

"I believe you know what I mean."

"I've worked for Crowley. He set me up to play on some public stage where he put on the Rites of Eleusis, some Greek thing. And we've done some private turns. Is that what you want?"

"Perhaps it is. Certainly nothing public. Tell me more of what you've done."

She looked at us with a hard set to her jaw. "That's enough

beating around for now. How much do you pay? Let's have it, or I'm off."

"Ten guineas, to begin," said Holmes. "And extras."

Her jaw relaxed and her eyes brightened. "Snow?"

"As much as you like."

"That's more like it. All right, Mr. Holmes, tell me what you want."

"I want you to cooperate with me, Leila. I am in an enterprise similar to Crowley's, but with a difference. You might say we are carrying out operations in opposition to each other."

"You mean good and evil?" said she, looking from one of us to the other. "Yes, you do, don't you."

"If you like, Leila. Those are not the terms I would use. But it is important for me to know the operations Crowley carries out, so I may counter them."

"Eh, he's a very devil, isn't he? You'd know it just to look at him. But then he starts coming on to you, and before you know it he's got you hooked. Even before he starts handing out the snow, I mean."

"I know exactly how you mean. So you can start earning your pay right now by telling me what you know."

"Ten guineas a go and all the snow I want? Right enough, Mr. Holmes. He has it coming to him."

"Do you know what is the purpose of his rites? What they are aimed at?"

"It's some sort of ritual magic, and I'm an essential part of it. He wants something out of me. I know what you're thinking, Mr. Holmes, and it's not just the pleasure of my flesh. He has a lot of high-sounding talk about the blood of the lion and the gluten of the eagle, and he means it. He does an enormous amount of chanting and concentrating, and he pushes himself to the limit. Something about eroto-comatose lucidity,* he says. But I'm the most impor-

---

* Crowley offered instructions on how this might be produced in his pamphlet, *De Arte Magica*. The larger philosophy behind it is explained by Crowley's disciple, Kenneth Grant, in his book, *Aleister Crowley and the Hidden God* (New York: Samuel Weiser, 1974).—Ed.

tant part of it, or something he wants out of me."

"And he has never told you what it is, or what it is for?"

"He says there is no need for me to know, in fact, that it's better if I don't. But I'll tell you what I think. It's something that gives him power, something he's trying to absorb from me."

"I can well believe that he wants power. But power for what purpose?"

She shook her head.

"Does it have something to do with a new religion?"

"Yes, he does have some sort of religion he's invented. Thinks he's God, he does. But then I expect he always did."

"Think, Leila, think. Something about the Era of the Father, and Era of the Child?"

"Something like that. Yes, I remember. He was raving about it one night. It came to him in Cairo about ten years ago, but he's keeping it secret until the time comes."

"The time for what?"

She looked at Holmes scornfully. "The time for him to reveal it, of course. What did you think I meant?"

"Whatever you are capable of comprehending," said Holmes. "Can you remember what he said happened in Cairo?"

"Sure. He had a revelation. Or rather she had it, his wife. The Scarlet Woman. That's me, too—his newest Scarlet Woman, I mean. She went into a trance, and quoted, and he wrote it down, or something like that. It's all written in a little red-leather-covered book of fine parchment. It's called the Book of the Law. He thinks it's the new Bible. He would, of course."

"Do you know what is in it?"

"In the book? Oh, all sorts of gibberish, I expect. I wouldn't remember if I'd heard it. Probably it says something about 'Do what thou wilt shall be the whole of the law.' He's always saying that. 'Do what thou wilt.' 'Do what thou wilt.' It's a sort of greeting he uses."

"And you remember nothing more?"

"Afraid not."

"Let me change the subject, then," said Holmes. "Have you ever heard him mention the names of people he knows?"

"I don't think so."

"Not Wittgenstein?"

She shook her head, beginning to look bored.

"Or Russell?" She shook it again.

"Keynes? Ramanujan?"

"Wait. Maybe."

"Which? Keynes or Ramanujan? or both?"

"The last one. The Indian bloke. He knew him."

"Do you remember what he said about him?"

"No. He talked about him a lot once, though. Seemed obsessed with him, almost. Then suddenly he stopped. I remember it because he just about went into a fit right before he stopped. If you ask me, this Ramanujan crossed him, and Crowley turned his magick against him. If he didn't poison him too. I wouldn't put it past him."

"Very good, Leila, very good indeed. Are you sure something won't come back to you now about the other names?"

"Yes, I've heard of one of them."

"Indeed," said Holmes, leaning forward. "Which?"

"Russell."

"Russell! What did Crowley say about him?"

"Oh, Crowley never said anything about him," said Leila, waving her hands. "I said *I've* heard of him. He's the bloke that goes about making speeches about the war that's going to happen, isn't he?"

"He is, Leila. He certainly is." Holmes slumped in his chair and pushed away his plate.

"Are we through for now?" said Leila. "Or do you want to start tonight? Where's your flat?"

"There is one more thing I would like to do tonight,' said Holmes. "We can do it right here. I want to put you into a trance."

"Into a trance?" She sat down again. "All right, that's slick. Let's go."

Holmes took his watch and swung it to and fro on its chain. Leila seemed familiar with the operation, for she stared at it and quickly became absorbed into herself, without a word of instruction. Within a minute her eyes had a glassy stare, and her lips began to move.

"Let the Scarlet Woman beware! If pity and compassion and

tenderness visit her heart; if she leave my work to toy with old sweetnesses; then shall my vengeance be known. I will slay me her child: I will alienate her heart: I will cast her out from men: as a shirking and despised harlot shall she crawl through dusk-wet streets, and die cold and an-hungered.

"But let her raise herself in pride! Let her follow me in my way! Let her work the work of wickedness! Let her kill her heart! Let her be loud and adulterous! Let her be covered with jewels, and rich garments, and let her be shameless before all men!

"Then will I lift her to pinnacles of power: then will I breed from her a child mightier than all the kings of the earth. I will fill her with joy: for I am divided for love's sake, for the chance of union. For pure will, unassuaged of purpose, delivered from the lust of result, is every way perfect."

She subsided for a few moments, and then began again.

"The ordeals thou shalt oversee thyself, save only the blind ones. Refuse none, but thou shalt know and destroy the traitors. I am Ra-Hoor-Khuit; and I am powerful to protect my servant. Success is thy proof; argue not; convert not; talk not overmuch! Them that seek to entrap you, to overthrow thee, them attack without pity or quarter; and destroy them utterly. Swift as a trodden serpent turn and strike! Be thou deadlier than he! Drag down their souls to awful torment: laugh at their fear: spit upon them!"

Her voice quieted and she was silent. Presently Holmes called to her:

"Leila! Speak again!"

Still she was silent, her eyes closed.

"Speak again! I demand it!"

She squirmed in her chair a little, but her eyelids did not open and her lips remained tight.

"I abjure you," said Holmes in a deep voice. "In the name of the higher powers, speak!"

"The study of the Book is forbidden," she said. "It is wise to destroy this copy after the first reading." She was silent again.

"In the name of the demon," cried Holmes, "say on!"

She spoke again. "Whosoever disregards this does so at his own risk and peril. These are most dire." Once more, she reverted to silence.

"Shall I speak his name?" said Holmes. "Shall I utter it loudly, for all to hear?"

"Those who discuss the contents of this Book are to be shunned by all, as centers of pestilence," came the reply. "The study of this Book is forbidden. It is wise to destroy this copy after first reading."

I had no idea what this extraordinary performance might mean,* and even Holmes sat silently for a few minutes. Presently Leila opened her eyes, and shook her head vigorously. She seemed very pleased with herself.

"Well, how was I? Did I say anything good?"

"You were most helpful, Leila. We are almost finished now. Tell me, have you seen Crowley recently?"

"Recently? Sure, I saw him yesterday."

"Yesterday? And what was he doing?'

"He's preparing for some big operation. But he's not doing it here in London, and he doesn't need me. He's leaving on a trip."

"Do you know where he is going?"

"He didn't say. He never does."

"And does he know you have come to see me?"

"Oh, yes. In fact, he left a message for you. A strange one, needless to say. Now, what was it?"

Holmes repressed a look of disgust. "It would be most interesting, my dear Leila. And it concerns your reward."

"Oh, I remember well enough. It was: 'If you wish to find me, look for me in Rabelais.' That's all."

"All right, Leila," said Holmes. "You may go now."

"Right. When do you want me again? Tomorrow night at your flat?"

"It will not be necessary. I think I have learned all there is to know."

She got up suddenly and glared at him, swinging her sequined handbag menacingly. "You blokes are all alike, aren't you?

---

* Elementary enough. Leila Waddell was in fact quoting from *The Book of the Law*, which was dictated to Aleister Crowley by a spirit in Cairo in 1904. The reader may examine the full text in a recent reprint (New York: Samuel Weiser, 1976), needless to say, at their own risk.—Ed.

Where's my reward? What was all that talk about ten guineas?"

"The ten guineas were for services implied but not yet rendered," said Holmes. "But I think this packet will pay you for your help this evening."

He handed across a small brown envelope.

Leila opened it and in one deft movement had it to her nose. "Good enough, Mr. Holmes. You're an all-right bloke after all. It's been a pleasure. You know where to reach me when you want me again."

Holmes sat silently after she had disappeared. "It seems the case has taken a dangerous turn," he said at last. "Leila Waddell has given us some useful information, and we should act upon it. Crowley's departure from London is disturbing. It means that he will be even harder to watch, and to control."

"Yes, and this great operation he is beginning. What can it mean? If only we knew more of his ring of accomplices. Keynes was once involved with him, but their battles over the drug deliveries prove they have broken off, and our chase after Keynes's apparition confirms that Crowley wishes to cast false suspicions upon him."

"Perhaps you are right, Watson. In any case, you are correct to remind us that we should think of the other members of the circle. I wonder where Wittgenstein is now? Crowley spoke of making a journey with him some day, and I think the man is deeper than his strange behavior suggests."

"We should not overlook Whitehead," I said. "He has opposed us from the start."

"Not to mention Russell himself," returned Holmes. "Is he not the ultimate candidate? With his pacifist godliness, and his intellectual purity, the perfect specimen of genteel humanity in all respects save the physical. Behind what better mask could a diabolical genius choose to hide?"

Holmes's joke was interrupted by a smooth laugh at my elbow. It was Keynes. He wore evening dress, and carried top hat and gold-topped cane in his hand. He seemed to have just finished a light supper and was on his way perhaps to some entertainment.

"What better mask indeed," he said. "But perhaps you gentlemen would like to see for yourselves?"

Holmes was already on his feet, and I struggled to follow.

"But where are we going?" I called after the receding figures of Holmes and Keynes.

"To Ludgate Prison," said Keynes. "Our friend Russell has been arrested."

CHAPTER 18

Russell in Jail

ussell's cell looked comfortable enough. It held a chair and table, with books, papers, and writing implements. We sat on the metal cot as the warder closed the barred door and went away.

"These conveniences are due to the kindness of Lord Balfour, the Foreign Secretary," said Russell with a wave of his hand. "And for the rest, it's rather less unpleasant than the months I spent at the crammer's before going up to the university."

"But why have they arrested you?" I cried. "Have they decided you are the murderer of Ramanujan?"

"Nothing so substantial as that," said Russell. "No, I am here for having uttered opinions before political meetings and in print. I proposed that a strike of munitions workers would be the most moral and effective way of preventing this self-destructive war. These opinions have been judged subversive under the Defense of the Realm Act, and the latter has taken precedence above the British tradition of freedom of speech and of the press."

"It is very regrettable," said Keynes, "although perhaps analogous to crying fire in a crowded theatre."

"Oh," said Russell, "I rather thought it might be like crying water in a burning one."

"You spoke once about the importance of your intuitions," said Holmes. "Have you had any such feelings recently, especially such as those you mentioned when you called us in regarding Wittgenstein?"

"For the most part I have been too busy to have any thoughts at all," said Russell. "Wittgenstein has not come back, and I have heard nothing of what has befallen him. I fear he may have some intention of joining the Austrian army when the outbreak of hostilities comes. But have you been able to make any progress in the matter, Holmes?"

"I have been swimming in murky waters," said Holmes. "Some landmarks though now begin to show, I think. That is why I asked if you might not have felt something impinging upon you from without."

"I confess that before I came here I felt I had been fighting an irresistible force that sapped all my energies. But I have given it a political interpretation only. There is nothing to match the momentum of the modern war machine, it seems, and its flywheels start turning long before the event. But I take it you mean something rather more personal, and of a psychic nature."

"I mean it entirely in an empirical sense, without interpretations. Subjective moods seem to be of the essence in this case."

"In that case, I should say that my mood has been dismal and depressed since I saw you last, and especially just the last few days before my arrest. My dreams have been troubled by formless things clawing from out of the void. Something has been pressing at me, if you like. But it can press me no farther. I have had a sudden reversal of that feeling since I entered these walls. I have everything that I want. There are no duties or interruptions. And now I hope to write a work on mathematical philosophy that my political activities had long prevented."

"You do seem well settled," said Keynes. "And the world shall have the benefit, when you come out, of another lasting work, instead of ephemeral pamphlets on a lost cause."

"For once, I may admit you are right on that topic," said Russell. "As things stand now, I should rather be in here than outside in the so-called great world. The moral level of the prisoners seems in no way inferior to that outside, although their intellectual level is somewhat lower, as evidenced by their having been caught. And there are impromptu amusements. When I was being lodged here, the admitting warder asked my religion. I told him I was an atheist. He asked me how to spell it, and remarked that he supposed there were many religions, although they all worshipped the same God."

Keynes and I could not keep from laughing, and even Holmes smiled.

"Careful, gentlemen, please," said Russell. "Just this afternoon I laughed aloud while reading a book of Lytton Strachey, and the warder came and reminded me sternly that this is a place of punishment."

"We leave you in good hands," said Holmes. "Let me ask one question before we go. I would like to know something of Rabelais."

"He is the great medieval French humorist and philosopher," said Keynes. "Have you never read *Gargantua and Pantagruel*?"

"Never," said Holmes.

"Then I recommend to you the chapter on rebuilding the walls of Paris," said Keynes. "The material they proposed to use is worthy of Aleister Crowley himself."

"Is there some reference in it," said Holmes, "to a motto such as 'Do what thou wilt'?"

"That is in a different part of the book," said Russell " 'Do what thou wilt' appears as the motto of the Abbey of Thelema, which is Rabelais' perfect institution of learning and worship. It contains the Renaissance ideal of all the worldly and spiritual arts and pleasures. And the name Thelema, of course, is the Greek for 'will.' "

We took our leave. On our way to Baker Street, Holmes stopped at the telegraph office and sent a large number of messages. He seemed lost in thought, and made no effort to explain himself.

We were nearly home when Holmes suddenly seemed to have changed his mind, and hailed a cab to drive us to Avenue Road. He would not answer my questions, but sat there in an attitude of deepening gloom.

The Theosophical Society was nearly empty that evening, no public lectures having been scheduled. Yet its lights were on everywhere, and the front door stood open. The front rooms were deserted, but the door to Mrs. Besant's office showed us a little crowd had gathered within. The young man with the pince-nez, Reverend Leadbeater, and several other intimates of the organization stood about in attitudes of dismay, for propped against the statue of the cat-goddess a cross-legged figure sat very stiffly. It was an elderly lady with red hair, and she ·vas dead.

"What has happened?" cried Holmes. "Where is Mrs. Besant?"

"Mrs. Besant has departed for a higher realm," said Reverend Leabeater, "leaving her outer sheath behind."

"This elderly lady? Mrs. Besant was a woman thirty years younger."

"Mrs. Besant was born in 1845," said the Reverend, "hence she was almost sixty-nine years old. It was her great spiritual vitality, constantly replenished by communion with the Other Side, that gave her a remarkable appearance of youthfulness. And it was while she was communing tonight, alone in her office, that she left this karmic sphere entirely, letting her body fall back into the ravages of time."

"When was she last seen alive?"

"At half-past seven this evening. She retired to her office, saying that she wished to meditate alone and that she felt it would be beneficial to her friends. She mentioned Mr. Russell in particular, and those who work on his side."

"Remarkable!" I cried. "The very hour we sat in Soho to interrogate Crowley's magic assistant. Can Crowley have struck here as well?"

"I do not doubt it," said Holmes. "Look here."

And he gestured to where the gramophone had stood in its corner—for it made no mocking echo now, but lay smashed upon the floor.

"A spirit much as Mrs. Besant's does not leave its body without releasing a flash of energy," said Reverend Leadbeater. "We heard a crash half an hour ago, and came in to find the gramophone had fallen and Mrs. Besant's spirit departed. It is not unusual—you may read of similar cases in my book, *Life After Death.** And indeed, this will make a wonderful instance for my current work, Volume Two of *The Hidden Side of Things.***

---

* Published by the Theosophical Publishing House (London and Madras) in 1912.—Ed.

** Published by the Theosophical Publishing House (London and Madras) in 1913.—Ed.

"Doubtless so," said Holmes. "Tell me, Watson, can your medical eye ascertain any other signs?"

"Nothing," I reported, for I had been examining the body. "It appears that a woman of approximately seventy years has died after some sudden exertion proved too much for her age."

We took our leave of Reverend Leadbeater, who seemed quite enthusiastic about the possibility of contacting Mrs. Besant's spirit in a séance, and rode grimly home.

"Now we can do nothing but wait," said Holmes. And he settled silently into his armchair with his pipe.

Next morning Holmes was sitting there still. A pile of telegrams had begun to collect on the table, and presently a messenger boy brought in more. Holmes scanned them quickly with a scowl.

"Crowley is not at Boleskin," he said, "and he is apparently not expected, for the house is closed up. And Inspector Clouzot wires that Crowley is not in Paris."

"He could be anywhere in the world," said I. "He is familiar with Mexico, the United States, India, China, Russia, North Africa. Indeed, anywhere."

"But he would not go that far," said Holmes. "His great plot is now coming to a climax, I think. That is why he is at pains that he should not be disturbed. But he would not wish to be too far from his victims. Telepathy, after all, is a finite process, limited by material space. If I am right, he has for targets the minds of all the great intellectuals, and that means he must stay in Europe. Look at these, Watson."

He handed across a clump of telegrams. They were dated Berlin, Paris, Zurich, Heidelberg, Copenhagen, and elsewhere.

"Remarkable!" I declared. "Einstein has recently fallen into a stupor, Niels Bohr is nodding, Poincaré in a fit, Bergson silent. Max Weber has for days been staring idly from his hotel window, and Marcel Proust has locked himself in a cork-lined room and refuses to come out."

"And Russell is locked in jail, Watson. His mind is too strong for Crowley to control, but he has been neutralized at least for the duration."

"Then this is serious, Holmes! We must find Crowley soon."

"We must proceed logically, Watson. Where would Crowley go? He must remain in Europe, that is clear. Under the circumstances, it would not be Germany or Russia, or the East. He is working upon the minds of the intellectuals, so let us assume he would act like an intellectual. Where do they go? A hideaway in Switzerland would be good, or for spiritual inspiration, Italy. And of course the south of France. Spain I think would not fit his intellectual concerns just now. But in Switzerland and France he would be too easy to locate. Their police systems are too good, and too hard to corrupt. No, I think we can count on his being near the Mediterranean, and the farther south the better, hence Calabria or Sicily. Now it only remains to inquire in underground circles there."

"In what sense do you mean underground?" said I.

"I mean in both the senses of criminality and the occult, Watson. Naples was once the center for occult studies, by reason of its proximity to the Arab world, and Sicily and the entire south of Italy are crossed with an enormous web of crime. I think that a telegram to my friend Lazaretti in Naples, together with the promise of a sufficient sum of money, will bring us the information we need. He must have a target for his search, and I believe that the name of the Abbey of Thelema will do."

He rang for Mrs. Hudson to bring a telegraph blank, and we settled down for another wait.

Late the following afternoon the answer came. Holmes read it quickly, and sprang to his feet.

"Come, Watson. There is no time to lose. Bring your service revolver."

"With all my heart," I declared. "Where are we going, Holmes?"

"To the village of Cefalu, in Sicily. And there, to Crowley's Abbey of Thelema."

CHAPTER 19

Confrontation of the Mages

On various trains we rumbled across Europe. No Phineas Fogg bound on a wager could have traveled harder and faster, nor more grimly and silently than Holmes and I. Calais, Paris, Lyons, Milan, Rome, Naples, Palermo—the stations rattled by.

At last a horse-drawn carriage hired in the seacoast village of Cefalu deposited us at a break in an old stucco wall halfway up a steep hill on the outskirts of town. The driver would take us no farther, and Holmes and I made what speed we could along an old stone roadway. The air was hot and moist, but evening was coming on, and black clouds hung in the sky promising the relief of rain.

Soon the Abbey came into sight. It was a long, plain building of cream-colored stone, with narrow windows rounded gracefully at the tops and set high in the walls. At the far end of the building, a high round tower with crenellated ramparts rose above the sea cliff.

Not a soul was to be seen as we passed through a garden of cypress and lemon trees. Once I heard a rustling in the bushes, and a receding titter like the sound of half-crazed pheasants. We came up the stone steps in silence. The great wooden doors stood open, and we passed inside. There in the hall stood Aleister Crowley.

"I cannot say I am pleased to see you, gentlemen," he said. He was wearing a plain white robe, and his shaven head was wrapped in a turban. "You have come at a most inopportune time. But perhaps it is all for the best. It may be, for both of us, Holmes, another ordeal to pass that leads on to higher things."

He turned and beckoned us to follow him through the great hall. The ceiling was high and airy, the walls completely plain save for the ribs of fine stone that arched upward to support the vault. The floor was set with a mosaic of tiles in blue and white and gold. The whole effect was cool and light. Here and there we passed a prayer rug laid upon the floor, and several low tables upon each of which sat a silver chalice. Holmes paused and picked up one. It was filled with a shiny white powder.

"Cocaine, is it not?" said Holmes.

"I leave it about so that visitors to the Abbey may learn restraint," said Crowley. "Take as much as you like. Only remember, a gram of it pure may prove fatal. Not for you, of course, Holmes, your capacity is higher."

Crowley smiled and went on. "Here at the Abbey of Thelema there is only one rule: Do what thou wilt. There are no external restraints. Whatever you desire, you may have. All variety of food, of perfumes, and drugs, and spirits, and potions, they are all here. All the pleasures of the flesh as well, none is forbidden. I have means to provide any music you wish to hear, any decoration or sight you wish to see, any entertainment or game you wish to play, be it infantile, dramatic, or intellectual."

"All in these bare rooms?" said Holmes.

"My house has many mansions," said Crowley. "Some here in this material form, others manifest as performances upon the theatre of the mind. The five senses are only avenues to the brain, as you know, and where one may achieve results by operating upon the brain directly, it is sometimes convenient to do so. But all this is only a means, not the end itself. The end is to discover your true will, and no longer to be led astray by petty cravings. Asceticism is not the way. To starve the flesh only makes it more ravenous, and one ends by doing interminable battle with oneself. I have a more profound method: to conquer the flesh by indulging it, to integrate body and soul by thoughtfully gratifying every whim, always being conscious of the result, until one's higher will becomes clear."

We had reached a circular room at the end of the hall. At the back a circular stairs led upward to the tower, and beside it hung a tapestry showing Crowley's familiar emblem:

At intervals around the walls there were huge mirrors, six in all, surrounding the room and reflecting each other back into infinity upon infinity. On the floor was a white sheepskin rug, and from the domed ceiling hung a large multitiered candelabrum, its tapers already burning in the twilight.

In the midst of the room was a dais, on which stood a tripod holding a cauldron of brass, and an altar of white marble upon which lay something covered with a blue cloth.

"It seems we have interrupted your proceedings," said Holmes.

"You have interrupted a Great Working," said Crowley. "It requires many months of unbroken concentration, and, correspondingly, it results in powers of the utmost consequence. The effects of breaking off before completion can be dire."

"Yet you have been here only a few days. Or can you carry on such concentration while you travel?"

"The disturbances of travel are in the balky nerves of the inexperienced," said Crowley. "I have been building up a crescendo of power for the past several weeks. You have noted the effects already, Holmes, or else you would not have come. I will not bother to inquire how you have found me. It evidences again your great intelligence, and intelligence is of the essence in this Working. So I shall count it good fortune to be interrupted in the midst of my greatest operation, if it means that I will be joined by a new partner, Sherlock Holmes himself."

"I should not care to join anything whose very purpose remains a mystery," said Holmes. "Pray explain yourself."

"There is much that cannot be told in advance. It was not told to me when I was first initiated. The greatest things you must learn by your own experience. But our minds are akin, Holmes, yours and mine. I will share with you what I know. When you understand what is involved, you will join with me, I am sure of it."

Holmes gestured with upturned palms and waited.

"We are entering a new era," Crowley continued. "This was revealed to me some years ago, in Cairo. Of course I am not the first to realize that the old order is dying, but few have had such a glimpse of the future. The old gods are dying, it is clear—Jehovah, Allah, and all the rest. So far our thinkers have noticed only the disintegration, the crumbling of outworn moral codes, the popular scorn for superstition and for traditions that no longer hold any meaning. Some find this hideous, that we now have no faith, except in the corrupting ambitions of money and politics, and the rumblings of lifeless machines. They do not realize that the old era must die in order for the new to be born, or that all this happened before.

"Every era, when it is young and strong, takes the form of a new religion. In ancient times, when men lived in tribes around little plots of land hoed by women, the religion worshipped the Mother. Then that religion died, and the age of the sword supplanted it, and along with it came the strength and discipline of the kings, and the religions of the Father. That is the age that is dying now. Along with it is dying the moral code of the group's iron discipline, with its hierarchy of master and slave, and its inner hierarchy of conscience and guilt. This is crumbling now, and those who look only backward into the past think that all morals are disappearing. They are wrong. They do not know they are witnessing the birth pangs of a new era, the Era of the Child. And it has fallen to me to proclaim its new religion.

"What does the new age worship? What is its moral code? The Mother was caring, the Father was stern. What is the Child? It is spontaneous and playful. It is the will untrammeled, finding itself without restraint, except the restraint of its own nature. Do what thou wilt is to be its law, a stern law in its own right, but it is the whole of the law.

"How, then, can we best make our way across this balance

point of world history? Can we avoid some of the buffeting of the wheel, as it spins in a new direction? We can, but only by concentrating all the powers of the new, and taking as much energy as we can from the old. That is why I have cultivated the greatest minds of our day. Some I have invited in person. Others I have been able to visit in spirit, as my powers have increased. And with each new accretion of mental power, my concentration grows stronger, and I can draw in more and more. So you can see the importance of this Great Working, Holmes. Through it I can change—through it, *we* can change—the entire world!"

"So that is it, Crowley. You ask the greatest men for their mental powers, and if they do not give them freely, you take them. Is that not a species of psychic vampirism?"

"I am as yet almost alone in living fully in the Era of the Child," said Crowley. "Remember, a child is generous, but also selfish. It is only the spontaneous impulses that count. And if this be vampirism, it is the true vampirism, the spiritual ideal behind the vulgar myth."

"Such are your aims," said Holmes. "What are your means? For the Era of the Child, they seem to center a great deal around women."

"Woman is essential indeed," said Crowley. "But she is not the Mother. She is the Shakti, the erotic force, the nearest emblem and source of the primal will that it is the nature of the Child to manifest."

"I see," said Holmes, with a look of distaste. "And hence your rites are necessarily erotic?"

"It is the only way to absorb the vital substance in its pure form. This is the most closely guarded secret in the rites, Holmes, save the actual names of invocation, but I give it to you as a sign of my trust. In the act of copulation, as you know, the female secretes various fluids. Fourteen of these are known to science, but it is the fifteenth and sixteenth that hold the vital powers. He who can stimulate a woman to that verge, and can absorb those final secretions, has taken into himself the quintessence of the quintessence, the life force itself. Such a man builds up psychic powers such as the world has rarely seen."

"Such powers can easily be used for ill," said Holmes. "Have you forgotten so soon the way you turned them against Srinivasa Ramanujan?"

"Your judgment is hasty," said Crowley. "Ramanujan died because of his tortuous resistance to his own impulses, not because of my will. Once established, the bond between master and chela cannot lightly be broken. Ponder this well, Holmes. Once the wills interlock, one becomes more than oneself. That is the meaning of the poetic image in which one calls up a demon, and then becomes enslaved to it."

"This was your justification to attack your old partner, John Maynard Keynes, I take it. And Mrs. Besant, did you not kill her as well?"

"Keynes was no partner of mine in any but a financial sense. He turned against me, once he saw how a drug business might be operated. He had no sense of its spiritual value. He even tried to interfere in my connection with Wittgenstein, by diluting his dosage and weaning him mechanically from the drug. His reasons for doing this I do not know, but they have something to do with his intellectual vanity regarding his university. As for Mrs. Besant, she was a fool. She opened up the hidden channels, but would not admit the real forces that lie beneath her sentimental feelings, the real erotic forces that are now entering the world in the Era of the Child. She stood as an obstacle in that channel once too often, and so it killed her."

"You seem to want to rise above the world, and have the rest beneath your feet," said Holmes. "In your hands, power is dangerous."

"Nonsense," said Crowley. "I wish to liberate the energies of the world. I do not wish to be a solitary king, but to be a star in a universal firmament. Every man and every woman is a star: so it says in the Book of the Law, and to realize this is my sworn goal."

"So you aspire, perhaps, at this moment. But your life pattern, to a dispassionate observer, would prove different."

"Think of what I am offering you, Holmes. With your talents, you can share all the greatness you can achieve. There are no fixed limits. Start on the path, and see how far you can go!"

"Enough," said Holmes. "I did not come to join you, but to bring you to justice."

"Very well," said Crowley. "We have reached the limits of words, and in your case, my dear Holmes, the limits of psychic persuasion as well. It is sometimes said very aptly that the strongest argument comes out of the barrel of a gun."

Evening had turned to night outside the high windows of the Abbey of Thelema. We all stood in silence, and into the stillness came the sound of the wind outside, and the swish of raindrops, and then the heavy splatter of water on the rocks. Then rain came pouring down in torrents. A heavy clap of thunder shook the building, and with it came a flash of lightning. When its brightness receded from our eyes, we saw that Crowley held something in his hands. It was a heavy-bore elephant gun, and its barrels were pointing at me.

"I know that Dr. Watson has a revolver in his pocket," said he, "and I know that you, Holmes, are carrying no weapon at all. Would you care to speculate about our respective capacities for discharging our weapons effectively?"

"I assure you," said Holmes, "that if you fire your first barrel against Watson, you will be dead before you have opportunity to fire the second. There is more than one martial art, as I should think you would know."

"Perhaps you are right," said Crowley, "and perhaps not. It makes an interesting wager. I once killed a Bengal tiger, and its mate, at extremely close quarters, when I unwittingly surprised them in a place that offered them no escape except over myself. But perhaps this is not the time for reminiscence. You would advise me, then, Holmes, to fire at you first, and to take my chances against Watson's slower draw and dubious aim?"

"By God, Crowley!" I declared. "You shall have the opportunity to regret that remark."

"I take it, my dear doctor, that you do not mean in my next incarnation," Crowley leered. "But to return to more serious discussion. I think my best course, my dear Holmes, is to keep my gun trained upon your friend, and to wager my life against his, to quote the best terms from your viewpoint. What do you say, my man? Or shall I make you another wager?"

Holmes was silent.

"It is this. Watson I shall keep under guard in a special place in this building designed long ago when the remnants of the Sicilian nobility kept up a secret resistance against the invading Aragonese. It is a room with a floor that may be suddenly released, pitching its inhabitant onto the rocks below. I think you know how this building is situated, and you should not doubt my word on this. Watson will be confined in this place, under my close surveillance, as hostage while you fulfill certain conditions."

"And what are these?"

"I shall not ask you to join me outright, Holmes, nor do I think that a mere exchange of pledges is sufficient for men of our intelligence. I wish only to establish certain external conditions, which should nevertheless be sufficiently binding. I shall require you, Holmes, to undergo an injection of a drug which I have devised, and while under its influence, to take part in a certain ceremony. It is a lengthy process, and it invokes spirits so potent that I have little doubt that with proper receptivity, no participant can ever be unaware of their calls again. You see that I make no moral claim upon you, Holmes. You shall simply experience the reality of the forces I have known. I myself first encountered them only by accident, and you see that now I am permanently their agent. And so shall you be, Holmes: earthly agent of the spirit that animates the era of the next two thousand years!"

"I would not do your bidding willingly," said Holmes. "Why do you think now that your drug shall do it for you?"

"You would not say so if you knew this drug," said Crowley. "It is nothing like cocaine, and hashish does not begin to compare with its lucidity. No, I assure you, it is a transcendental experience in itself. Anything that happens to you under its influence is magnified a thousandfold. You will realize how the universe is a creation of your mind, and, at the dosage which I have prepared, you will see the white light that once was called God. Nay, I have full confidence in it. Once you pass through that door, you will never come back. That is all I ask, Holmes. One injection will be enough. When the ceremony is finished, Watson will be released."

With a sweep of his free hand, Crowley pulled aside the cloth upon the altar. There lay a glass syringe with a silver needle and a short plunger. It contained a tiny dose of clear liquid.

"How far you are from the mystical heights," said Holmes mockingly. "Yours is truly an artificial paradise, Crowley. The sages and masters of old rose above such worldly things."

"Do not make me think less of you by displaying such ignorance," said Crowley. "Surely you have heard of the philosophers'
stone, in the search for which so much treasure was expended. It
was not, as the vulgar supposed, merely a device for transforming
lead into gold. It transformed the impurities of the human body
and mind into the clear crystalline light of the realized will. This is
what magick is about, my friend. It takes us not merely from earth
to heaven, but brings heaven down to earth. It makes us realize
they are one. Mind and matter, body and soul, light and darkness,
they are the same. On the highest level, this needle is identical
with the energy of the cosmic void."

"Very well," said Holmes. "I will accept your wager. Tell me,
does your drug take long to act?"

"Injected into the blood stream, or even within the skin, it is
practically instantaneous. It is by far the most potent drug ever
known to mankind."

"And when shall we begin?"

"As soon as Watson has delivered up his revolver," said Crowley. He poked the rifle at me meaningfully. "For the moment, we
are still in the realm of grosser contingencies."

"Do as he says, Watson," said Holmes.

I looked at Holmes for some further sign, but his face was
impassive. I drew the revolver from my pocket and tossed it to the
floor. With a deft movement, Crowley had it in his free hand, and
sent it arching through a seaward window.

"Now if you will be so good as to step to my left, Dr. Watson."
He indicated a corner formed where the doorway to the great hall
jutted into the room, so that I stood between an angle of wall and
the dais upon which stood the altar.

"Now I may dispense with this cumbersome weapon," Crowley continued. He quickly dropped the rifle into a cranny beneath
the tapestry at the rear, and grasped instead a long tasseled cord
that hung from the ceiling. I had supposed it to be a bellpull.

"No, it is not a bellpull," said Crowley, evidently reading my
mind again. "It is the cord that releases the floor I spoke about.
Just there where you stand near the door, with its sheer walls
offering no handhold, that is the place to which I referred just
now. What better place for an ingenious Sicilian to mount his

ultimate defense, than here at the threshold of his inner chamber? I would not advise you to think of moving at all, Dr. Watson, until this operation is completed. I need not hold the cord, I think, but it is easily within my reach. I am exceedingly quick in matters of this sort, and I have the added advantage of being able to anticipate your every inclination."

Crowley surved the scene with a look of evident pleasure. "And now, Holmes, if you will kindly advance to the altar and inject yourself, the operation can begin. I believe you know the method."

We stood frozen for a minute as our tableau flickered in the lights of the candelabrum overhead: I to the left, Holmes to the right, Crowley in the center behind his dais like some ghastly Christ in a medieval triptych. The deadly cord hung a few feet from his hand. The lightning flashed again, and we saw that a fourth figure had been added, standing beside me in the doorway. It was Wittgenstein, and in his hand he held a revolver pointed squarely at Crowley's heart.

CHAPTER 20

The Lord of the Ring

Wittgenstein's unruly hair stood out in all directions, and the lightning behind him gave him the silhouette of some creature from an age beyond our own. His face was strangely contorted, and his eyes seemed to glow with a yellow light.

"I do not stand idly by to see my people exterminated," he declared at last. "I have tracked you for a year, Crowley, since the cowardly murder you committed at Cambridge. Now in one second, you yourself will be dead."

"Perhaps I shall," said Crowley. "But if so, you will have upon your conscience the murder of an innocent man. Can you face that, Wittgenstein? Ramanujan's death is morally upon his own head."

"Nonsense," said Wittgenstein. But his face contorted again, and his hands began to twitch.

"Nay, it is so," Crowley went on. "It was Ramanujan himself who asked me to induct him into the Order of the Silver Star, and he underwent many rites at his own behest. It is he that asked for more and more of his favorite drug. You know my philosophy. One must find one's own true will. If I am asked, I supply the means, be they physical or spiritual. I give unstintingly, I hold nothing back. If one cannot abide the consequences, or wishes to twist and turn in midstream, it is not my fault. Ramanujan

148

invoked a demon, and he had not the will to control it. That is all."

Wittgenstein twitched silently for a minute. The seconds passed.

"No, you are wrong," he said finally, in a high-pitched voice. "Ramanujan was a seeker after truth. He did not indulge himself. It is you who increased the dosage of heroin to the point where it sapped his strength. I knew the man. I did not like him, but I know he was as pure in his own inclinations as a Hindu saint."

"Do not be so sure," said Crowley. "There is much beneath the surface of every human being. The bluest puritan may be an eroto-maniac under the skin. I knew a painter of elegant ladies in Vienna, who has a most peculiar method. He sketches the face, and then in the privacy of his studio he draws the body nude, with the *pubis* rendered in minute detail, before he hides the whole in a gaudy pattern of clothes. Perhaps you know him, my dear Ludwig. His name is Klimt, and I have seen the picture he did of your sister."

Wittgenstein uttered a howl of rage. He drew back his arm, and hurled his revolver violently in Crowley's face.

Quick as a cat Crowley had the tasseled cord-pull and gave it a sudden jerk.

But it was not the floor that fell, but the candelabrum, crashing in the midst of the room and plunging us into darkness. Then the lightning flashed, and I saw Crowley's hand close upon the syringe. In an instant, he had thrown himself at Wittgenstein.

My aging bones had not moved so fast in many a year. For I hurled myself against the philosopher, knocking him away. And then I felt a sharp pang, and a sudden rush in my blood. Crowley's needle had caught me in the arm.

The shock of the sensation was like nothing I had ever expected. I can only say, with medical retrospect, that it was like the sensation in the *glans penis* at the moment of *ejaculatio*, only it rapidly spread throughout my entire body in one hot glorious wave of molton pleasure. I felt suddenly detached from the world and all its concerns, and I thought that I must die.

I slumped to the floor. I heard muffled cries, as from a great distance, and the air pressed upon me like a glassy ocean, in which murky figures were swimming about. His exit cut off, Crowley rushed across the room, and Holmes and Wittgenstein

after him. I heard them clamoring, far away, up the stairs to the
tower. Later I learned they had climbed to the roof overlooking
the sea cliff. Crowley had a good start, and, natural climber that
he was, beat them to the top by several seconds. As Holmes and
Wittgenstein came through the door, Crowley was already upon
the battlements, and they caught only a glimpse before he
jumped. But even in my swoon, I could not escape the meaning of
that terrible cry, as the body hurtled five hundred feet into the
tides below.

Bertrand Russell

Ludwig Wittgenstein

that he is living alone in a hut on the coast of Norway, and other reports that he is working as a house builder in the hills of Austria. Still another says that he has become a gardener in a monastery."

"At any rate, it closes the case," said Keynes. "Poor Ramanujan is dead. Hardy has left for Oxford, Whitehead for Harvard. Moore devotes himself to the editorship of *Mind*, and our friend Russell here is usually abroad, visiting and lecturing in Russia and China and wherever new social experiments are afoot."

"All the better," said Russell, "since my patriotism does not weigh heavily enough in the intellectual scales of Trinity College. They have deprived me of my Fellowship."

"So we are most of us gone, all gone," said Keynes. "The ring is broken. But justice has been done. That blackguard Crowley fell to his death from his tower in Sicily, rather than fall into your clutches, Holmes."

"The body was never found," Holmes remarked.

"No, the body was not found," returned Keynes. "But the probabilities are exceedingly high that the waves washed it out to sea, and also it is probable that the Sicilians did not expend much effort in searching for it. And probabilities, gentlemen, are the only sure method we have in this world in which we live."

"Not entirely," said Holmes. "I happen to have positive intelligence that Aleister Crowley is still alive."

"Alive, Holmes?" I exclaimed. "How is this possible? Crowley jumped from the wall at the top of a sheer cliff five hundred feet high. No one could survive such a fall."

"You overlook a fact," said Holmes, "that Crowley himself was exceedingly fond of enunciating: he was, indeed, the world's greatest mountain climber. He had been observed making greater miracles than that in the Alps, and in the Himalayas. To the expert eye, your sheer vertical cliff might reveal an abundance of footholds and handholds. And furthermore, I have heard reports of him."

"Indeed," said Russell. "Where?"

"In America. He is using various aliases: Gurdjieff, Gatsby, Burroughs, Leary, and others. Yet with all this, I foresee that we shall not be able to catch him."

"Why not?" said Keynes. "How can you be so sure?"

"I too have my methods," said Sherlock Holmes.

Epilogue

It was not until after the Great War that I heard the termination of the case of the philosophers' ring. By chance, strolling with Holmes on a spring morning, we encountered Bertrand Russell and John Maynard Keynes coming up St. James' Street. Keynes was returning from the Treasury, where he had just devised the financial measures that should have served to keep Britain prosperous through the next trying decades.

It was Russell who mentioned our philosophers' case.

"The future of philosophy is secured, Holmes. With your help, we have come through. Wittgenstein has sent me at last the manuscript of his book, and I am now seeing it through the press."

"And is it all that you expected?" said Holmes.

"It is a most curious work," said Russell. "I do not know if what it says is true, but I can see no way in which it is clearly false, and I am certain that it is important."

"Quite so," said Keynes. "Quite a load of importance indeed, for a work which is a mere seventy pages long, and consisting entirely of short paragraphs numbered from 1.01 to 7. Of course in our translation it is twice as long, as Wittgenstein insisted that nothing of his may appear in English without the German original being available on the facing page."

"So he is still suspicious as ever," said Holmes. "But tell me, how is our friend Wittgenstein?"

"He has disappeared again," said Russell. "I have heard reports

151

Annie Besant

Aleister Crowley

John Maynard Keynes

Lytton Strachey and Virginia Woolf

Leila Waddell, "The Scarlet Woman"